By Nessa L. Warin

NOVELS
Sauntering Vaguely Downward
Stamp of Fate
Storm Season
Syrah
To Dream, Perchance to Live

NOVELLAS
The Stars Are Brightly Shining

Published by DREAMSPINNER PRESS
http://www.dreamspinnerpress.com

*Shae,
Enjoy! Thanks
for everything.*
♡
Nessa L. Warin

SYRAH

NESSA L. WARIN

Dreamspinner Press
5032 Capital Circle SW
Ste 2, PMB# 279
Tallahassee, FL 32305-7886
USA
http://www.dreamspinnerpress.com/

This is a work of fiction. Names, characters, places, and incidents either are the product of the author's imagination or are used fictitiously, and any resemblance to actual persons, living or dead, business establishments, events, or locales is entirely coincidental.

Syrah
Copyright © 2013 by Nessa L. Warin

Cover Art by Brooke Albrecht
http://brookealbrechtstudio.blogspot.com

Cover content is being used for illustrative purposes only
and any person depicted on the cover is a model.

All rights reserved. No part of this book may be reproduced or transmitted in any form or by any means, electronic or mechanical, including photocopying, recording, or by any information storage and retrieval system without the written permission of the Publisher, except where permitted by law. To request permission and all other inquiries, contact Dreamspinner Press, 5032 Capital Circle SW, Ste 2, PMB# 279, Tallahassee, FL 32305-7886, USA.
http://www.dreamspinnerpress.com/

ISBN: 978-1-62798-030-2
Digital ISBN: 978-1-62798-031-9

Printed in the United States of America
First Edition
August 2013

LIKE all books, this book was not written in a vacuum. There are people and businesses I'd like to thank for their influence and support.

First, Royce's wine shop and the tastings he hosts are based on a real wine shop: The Wine Merchant located in Cincinnati, Ohio. It was at their tastings that I fell in love with wine, and there that I conceived the idea of a customer stumbling into a wine shop and falling in love with the owner.

I would like to thank my friend Dan, who works at The Wine Merchant, for his invaluable advice whenever I had questions about what wine I should use or how to describe something. He gave me ideas and tastes and brought a whole additional level of realism to the story.

I want to thank Beau Schemery for writing the description of Syrah that appears in the front of this book. His description taught me things about one of my favorite wines, and it fits the tone of this book perfectly.

I need to thank Ariel Tachna both for introducing me to the tastings at The Wine Merchant and for encouraging me every step of the way with this book… even when I was writing on my phone while I should have been working at the former Evil Day Job.

Thanks to Stella Harris for Portland-picking this book. I've visited the city a few times and adore it, but nothing compares to living there, and she was gracious enough to read an early draft of this and help me out.

Finally, thanks to everyone at Dreamspinner Press. Through working with them, both as an author and at my new, *So*-Not-Evil-Except-In-The-Most-Delicious-Ways Day Job, they've become a family. My life has changed in such a positive way because of Dreamspinner. I have a job I love, working with people I adore every day. The Editorial Department has helped me improve my writing so much (though I fear I will never fully grasp commas). The Art Department has given me fantastic covers for all my books. And I get to work with some of the most phenomenal, positive, giving people I've ever met.

A girl really can't ask for more than that.

SYRAH: A versatile and elegant grape that can be found as a component to refined and sophisticated blends in France's Côtes du Rhône to the big, powerful, single-varietal fruit bombs of the Barossa Valley in Australia, and everywhere in between.

Known also by Sirah and Shiraz, Syrah is a dark-skinned grape that produces complex and flavorful, full-bodied wines. The wines are characterized by aromas of dark berries, pepper, cocoa, and sometimes lavender. Even in blends, the pepper and dark berry notes show through, and they're echoed on the palate. In Australia's warm southern growing regions, these flavors become almost jammy.

Syrah is a beautiful grape that has been embraced by the new and old world winemaking community alike. And though it can exhibit quite differently from area to area, one thing is certain: Syrah is always delicious.

1

THE jingling of the door chimes startled Royce from his contemplation of the unusual snow falling outside, covering the roads and sidewalks faster than the deicer could melt it. He turned, a ready smile on his face as he tried to hide his surprise that he was getting a customer now—after nearly two hours without any and an hour of wondering if he should close like every other business in Portland—and rested his hands on the wooden counter he'd been leaning against. "Welcome to All Corked Up. Can I help you find something?"

"I am so glad you're here." The customer pulled off a pair of black leather gloves and dropped them on the counter next to the computer before he pulled down the red scarf wrapped around his face and grinned. "The other place I tried was closed because the roads are freezing, and everywhere else is completely out of my way. I thought I was going to have to get wine from the grocery store, and that would have been a disaster."

"Their selection isn't horrible," Royce offered diplomatically as he looked up—and up—to meet the man's eyes. His heart twisted a little as he took in the guy's chiseled good looks, and he reminded himself that hitting on a first-time customer was a really bad idea, despite the mostly accepting atmosphere of Portland. Royce wasn't in the closet, per se, but he didn't walk around advertising he was gay either. Conservatives liked to drink wine too, and unless they came in ranting about things that would offend him, his employees, or his customers, Royce didn't mind selling it to them. "If you know what you're looking for, you can usually find something worth buying there."

"That's the problem." The man twisted his lips up into a wry grin, and Royce's stomach flipped. He had *dimples*. "I don't know what I'm looking for." He leaned forward, resting his hands on the counter, and looked Royce straight in the eyes. "You have to help me. *Please*."

"I can try," Royce assured him. He could easily guess what the man wanted help with, but even if he was wrong, he wasn't about to turn away a tall, built guy with hazel eyes and a gorgeous smile. "What are you looking for?"

"Um…." The guy rubbed at the back of his neck and ducked his head. "Wine?"

Royce pointedly looked over his store. The counter he was standing behind was mostly devoted to the computers he used as registers, but there were open cases of wine behind it and wine accessories on either side and between the two computers. In the back corner was a wooden bar with a refrigerator underneath and a few bottles of resealed red wine sitting on the counter behind it. Three of the walls were devoted to shelves full of wine organized by region and type, bins in the middle held more bottles, and several cases were arranged in artful displays not too far from the bar. There was a cooler along one wall, holding prechilled whites and rosés, and the other room, where he held tastings, had another bar and several cases of wine stacked along the walls.

"I think I can help with that," he said dryly when his gaze returned to the man on the other side of the counter. "What kind of wine would you like?"

3

"Yeah, see, that's the problem. I don't—" He shook his head. "I like wine. It's just, I tend to hang out with people who prefer beer, you know? I usually only have wine with my family or get whatever the server recommends at a restaurant if I want to splurge. But my sister-in-law is hosting Christmas dinner tonight, and she always brings a bottle of something that tastes *amazing* with whatever my mom cooks for dinner."

Royce chuckled. "And she told you to bring the wine this time?"

"Well, my mom did, but yeah. Karen is making the ham and the green bean casserole and my mom and my sister are bringing the other sides. I would bring one too—I have this amazing spinach casserole that I love to make and sometimes I even actually mash potatoes—but we've been really busy at work and I've been pulling extra shifts. I knew I wouldn't have time to cook, so Mom told me to just bring the wine. Only, I forgot last week and I ended up working this morning. Everywhere is closing early because it's Christmas Eve and it's snowing. I can't just bring a bottle I grab at random off the grocery store shelf to *Karen's*."

His chest was heaving when he finished, and Royce's brain was scrambled from trying to keep up. "Do you always talk this much?" He didn't mean to say it aloud, but the words left his mouth before his brain could tell his lips it wasn't a good idea. "Shit. Sorry. I don't usually—"

The guy chuckled self-deprecatingly. "It's fine. I know I can be a little, ah, overwhelming." He flashed a grin that made Royce's heart thud wildly in his chest. "I guess you don't usually have customers coming in and spilling their life stories to you?"

"Not *before* they've sampled a few at the tasting bar."

The guy's chuckle turned into a full-fledged laugh. He threw his head back, clutched at his stomach, and almost smacked his forehead on the counter when he bent over. His whole body shook, and it was a good minute before he managed to look up and meet

Royce's eyes again. "I'll try to keep that in mind. No life stories sober. Got it."

Royce actually *wanted* to hear this guy's life story, but saying so might come across as a little creepy. "I don't mind," he said instead, flashing what he hoped was an indulgent grin. "It's more entertaining than watching the snow fall."

"I don't know." The guy peered around Royce to look out the window behind him. "It's coming down hard. Might be a good show."

"From the safety of my living room, sure. Not when I have to think about going out in it later." If things went to plan, he wouldn't have to step outside at all until the snow stopped, but at the very least he'd have to go out and clear the sidewalk later. It was a liability to leave it icy.

"How much later?"

The sign on the door said eight, but with the way the snow was falling, Royce knew he wouldn't stay open another four hours. "I was thinking about closing when you came in, actually."

"You should. Well, I hope you'll help me first, because I really *can't* go to Karen's with something I grab at random from the grocery store, but after I leave. When I leave. Whatever."

He looked so earnest Royce had to laugh. "I might."

"Great!" The guy rubbed at the back of his neck. "So, uh, what should I take to dinner tonight? Please tell me you have some ideas."

Royce did. He needed more information before he gave any suggestions. He would *really* like it if this particular customer became a regular—for the eye candy if nothing else—but he definitely had a few bottles in mind. "You mentioned ham and green beans. What else are you having?"

"Mom's making sweet potatoes, and Megan—that's my sister—is making my spinach casserole. I think she's bringing cranberry sauce too, but just the kind from a can. Oh, and my dad bought dessert. Chocolate cream pie and blueberry cobbler, I think."

He held his hand out over the counter. "I'm Shawn, by the way. I figured since I'm telling you half my family's names you should know mine too."

Royce took it and shook firmly, marveling at the way Shawn's hand wrapped completely around his. "Royce Wilkinson. Owner of this place."

"No shit? Really? And you're working on Christmas Eve?"

"It's not exactly fair to expect my employees to work today if I'm not willing to." Royce headed around the counter so he could show Shawn through the store. "Besides, they all have family in town. Mine isn't supposed to get here until about eight thirty tonight. If they're not delayed," he added wryly, glancing over his shoulder at the snow blanketing the ground. "It might be later, the way this is falling."

"Are they flying or driving?" Shawn fell into step as Royce led the way to the back of the store.

"Driving, thankfully. If they were flying, I don't know that they'd get in at all. At least if they have to stop, they can find a motel and not be stuck in an airport." Royce stopped in front of the section of French wines. "Do you have a preference for white or red?"

Shawn looked flummoxed. "Um. No? I mean, I usually drink red, but I like white too. What do you think we should have?"

"Personally, I would suggest red. But I can find a white that would go well with your meal too, if you'd prefer." Royce crouched down in front of the shelf, then twisted to look up at Shawn. He looked like a giant from this angle. "There are several of either that would work well with ham."

"I think everyone coming drinks red, so let's go with that." Shawn crouched down next to Royce, knocking their knees together and almost sending Royce tumbling to the ground. He grabbed Royce, steadying him, and Royce had to work hard to focus on the wine in front of him instead of the warm hand curled around his shoulder.

"Okay, well, I would recommend either a Rasteau, the Meiomi Pinot Noir, or the Atteca Grenache," Royce said, pointing to three bottles on the lower shelves. "The Rasteau is the lightest, best if you have people who prefer whites or rosés, and the Meiomi Pinot is our most popular of these, but for what you're having, I'd pick the Grenache."

Shawn looked at all three bottles, pulled them off the shelf one at a time, rolled them over, and read the descriptions on the back. "This one?" he asked, holding up the last one.

"It's what I'm serving tomorrow."

"Will it go with dessert too, or should I get a different bottle for that?"

"For chocolate cream pie and blueberry cobbler? I'd recommend either a Pinot Noir or a Syrah." Royce pointed to a bottle of Pinot Noir just above his head. "This is one of my favorite Pinots. Very good, but less expensive than the Meiomi, by about ten bucks a bottle, so for the money…."

"I'll take it." Shawn grabbed the bottle of HobNob Pinot Noir off the shelf, along with two bottles of Atteca Grenache. "Karen is the only one who really knows a lot about wine. My mom wouldn't notice if I brought wine in a box."

Royce shuddered, glad Shawn at least knew enough not to get that, even if he was otherwise clueless. "Wow."

"Yeah. I didn't even like that back in college. I'm not bringing it to Christmas dinner." Shawn flashed a grin as he climbed to his feet and held up the bottles. "Is this going to be enough? There are six of us drinking. Maybe seven if Meg brings her boyfriend."

"Depends on how much you want to drink." Royce said as he eyed the bottles thoughtfully. "That'll give you about two glasses each with dinner and one with dessert."

"Grab me another one of each." Shawn nudged Royce's shoulder as he tucked the bottles back into his arms. "I'd rather have too much than not enough. It'll keep, right?"

Royce grabbed the bottles off the shelf and started back toward the register. His shoulder was tingling where Shawn had bumped him, and he couldn't stop smiling despite the knowledge that he might never see this particular customer again. "If you don't open them. Or you can seal them with a vacuum sealer and they'll keep for about a week."

"Do you sell those?"

Royce set the bottles on the counter. "Yeah, but your sister-in-law probably already has one if she likes wine."

"Not with my luck." Shawn set the bottles he was carrying down and turned to look at Royce with a teasing smile on his lips. "Besides, aren't you supposed to want to sell me things?"

"I think you're buying enough." Royce chuckled as he crossed to the shelf and grabbed one of the vacuum sealers with a spare plug. "But if you *really* want to spend more, far be it from me to stop you."

Shawn took the package, read the back, and tossed it on the counter. "Hey, if I buy this, I'll have to come back and buy more wine some time so I know I'm getting my money's worth out of it."

"Oh well, in that case, I think I need to insist that you buy it." Royce couldn't stop grinning as he moved around the counter and pulled up the computer. "Did you want to create an account here? I send out newsletters with specials and details on our upcoming wine tastings."

"Is it from you personally?"

Shawn's smile made Royce's knees go week. He leaned heavily on the counter and reminded himself that just because the guy was friendly, gorgeous, and hadn't mentioned bringing any sort of significant other to Christmas dinner, it didn't mean he was available or interested. He was a customer, not someone Royce was chatting up in the bar. "No," he managed, "it's from the store."

"Shame." Shawn gave his e-mail address anyway, revealed that his last name was Neale, and paid with a credit card. While Royce packed up the wine in a carry box, Shawn pulled his gloves back on. "Thanks." He curled his fingers around the handle of the box. Royce swore that he felt a little tingle even through Shawn's gloves. "Really. You saved me from utter embarrassment."

"Just doing my civic duty."

"Right. It's so helpful to society for you to stay open on a snowy day just so I can bring the right wine to my Christmas dinner."

"Well, if you were embarrassed, who knows what you might do? It could be bad."

"Oh, absolutely." Royce managed to keep a straight face longer than Shawn, but he lost it the minute Shawn started laughing, and ended up doubled over the counter despite the fact that it wasn't that funny. Shawn's laughter was impossible to resist.

It was a few minutes before he was able to straighten. "Enjoy your Christmas dinner," Royce said.

"Thanks." Shawn took the wine and grinned. "You too. I'll, uh, see you around." He pushed the scarf back up over his face and disappeared out the door.

Royce watched him go with a fond smile on his face. It wasn't likely that he meant what Royce hoped he meant, but even repeat business would be good. And repeat business from Shawn? Even the idea of it made staying open through the snow worth every bit of the hassle it was going to take to get home.

2

A WEEK later, Shawn stood on the sidewalk outside All Corked Up, contemplating the building as if it held all the answers to life's questions. It was a two-story brick building, unremarkable on the outside, only distinguished by the bright purple canopy over the entrance and the artistic decorations on the windows. Currently, they consisted of snowmen sharing a champagne toast with fireworks in the background, but last week the scene had been reindeer around a Christmas tree, and Shawn remembered seeing other scenes when he'd driven by in the past. It wasn't spectacular artwork, but it was good, and as he walked inside, he wondered if Royce painted them himself or left it to one of his employees.

The man standing behind the counter was short and stocky, with spiked light-brown hair and arm muscles that were defined even through the long sleeves of his shirt. His face was rugged rather than classically handsome, but he was easy on the eyes, and Shawn would have wanted to look if he hadn't been hoping to see Royce.

"Hey, how are you doing?" the man asked, leaning over the counter to grin at Shawn.

"Good." Shawn unzipped his coat as he stepped further into the store. The Christmas Eve snow had melted by the day after Christmas, replaced by Portland's frequent rain, but the slight temperature difference necessary to keep the precipitation from freezing didn't mean it was warm. Shawn was wet and cold from the time he'd spent on the sidewalk psyching himself up to come inside, and his throat burned with disappointment as he realized it might have been for nothing. "Is Royce here?"

"Not right now, but I can help you with everything he can."

Shawn doubted that, but he couldn't tell Royce's employee that he'd come back hoping to flirt with his boss and see if the interest he thought he'd noticed was real. "He helped me pick out some wine for Christmas, and my family was so impressed I've been instructed to bring some to New Year's."

"But you're secretly clueless, right?"

"Not so secretly." Shawn laughed. "My family knows I'm not great with wine. But it was either agree to get it again or share the secret and inflict my mother on you guys." He'd actually volunteered, thrilled at the chance to see Royce again, but neither Royce nor his employee needed to know that.

"Usually, we like it when people recommend us, but I'm gonna guess not sending your mother here is a good thing."

"Well, I'll send her in eventually, I'm sure. I just want to make sure you guys can handle her first. I like this place and she's... intense." Shawn laughed, though it felt forced. The man helping him seemed pleasant enough, but he didn't feel the spark that had brought him back hoping to find Royce again.

"You want to make sure we like you before you let her influence our opinions, you mean." The man knocked on the counter as he walked around it. "I'm on to you."

"Yep. That's it." Shawn rocked back on his heels. "You've caught on to my nefarious scheme."

"Nefarious, huh?" The man took a step back, though his obviously mischievous expression made it clear to Shawn it was just a game. "I'm not sure I can sell you wine if you admit to a nefarious scheme. We tend to draw the line at devious around here."

"Come on!" Shawn took a step forward, playing along. The relaxed atmosphere of All Corked Up was a nice break from the stuffy formality of the tiny restaurant he worked in, and he wasn't going to turn down the opportunity to enjoy it. "I won't tell. I promise."

"You say that, but what if tricking me is part of this nefarious scheme? You'll get me on your side and then—bam! Bye-bye, Clint."

"It's not *that* nefarious of a scheme. I'm just not sure devious is the right word either." Shawn hooked his thumbs in his jean pockets as he regarded Clint with a mock-serious expression. "What if I just don't describe it at all? Shawn's Scheme has a nice ring to it, don't you think?"

Clint's eyes widened slightly, and he glanced toward the back of the shop before looking Shawn up and down. "*You're* Shawn? The Shawn who came in on Christmas Eve?"

"Yeah." Shawn drew out the word as he took a step back, a little thrown by Clint's sudden intensity.

"Damn." Clint snapped his fingers. "Guess that means I should behave. Wait right there."

"Uh. Okay." Shawn didn't know what Clint was up to, but by the time he thought to ask, Clint was already at the back of the store.

He yanked open a door Shawn hadn't noticed before and leaned through the doorway with one hand on the knob and the other on the frame. "Royce! Get down here! I've got someone you want to see!"

"Just a minute," Royce called back, his voice familiar to Shawn even a week after their brief meeting. "I need to—Crap! Catch her!"

An orange, black, and white streak shot between Clint's legs, ricocheted off the far wall, and headed toward the front of the shop without slowing. Clint let go of the door and raced after it with surprising agility, but he every time he got close, the animal changed directions and stayed just out of his grasp.

"Kirra!" Royce appeared in the doorway and nodded once at Shawn before turning his attention to Clint. "Her name is Kirra, Clint."

"I don't think she knows that yet. Or maybe she just doesn't care." Clint lunged, almost hitting a stack of wine boxes. His fingers brushed over Kirra's back, but she flattened at the last second, evading him once again. He cursed and glared as he climbed back to his feet. "Where the hell did you get her, Royce? She's *crazy*!"

"She's a kitten." Royce stepped into the room, closed the door behind him, and calmly looked at the tiny calico kitten crouched behind a stack of boxes. "It would be weird if she weren't crazy."

"She's crazier than most." Clint tried to grab her again, missed. She ran toward Royce, dodged when he reached for her, and headed toward the front of the shop.

By sheer luck, Shawn managed to snag her as she tried to run past. "Gotcha."

The kitten squirmed in Shawn's grip, revealing a patch of dark fur in the shape of a paw print on her stomach. When that failed to free her, she looked straight at Shawn, her green eyes shining brightly out of the mask of orange and black fur that stretched around her eyes and down her nose. "Eh eh!"

Shawn blinked as he held her out toward Royce. "She chirps."

"Yeah." Royce took the kitten and cradled her against his chest. "Thanks."

"Cats don't chirp. They meow." Shawn eyed the kitten warily, pretending he was much more disturbed by the odd sound she made than he actually was. It was safer to focus on the way she pawed at

Royce's shirt than on how well the dark blue material complemented his eyes.

It was better for Shawn to look at the cat overall if he wanted to avoid embarrassing himself. He'd found Royce attractive last week, when he'd been neatly groomed, but today, with stubble on his chin and his hair sticking out in all directions, he was irresistible. If Shawn looked up, he'd lose himself staring into Royce's blue eyes or at the tiny cleft in his chin, and he'd be so mortified when caught he wouldn't want to come back.

"Kirra chirps." Royce shrugged and shifted the kitten in his arms. "It's unconventional, I know, but she's an unconventional kitten."

"She's batshit insane, you mean." Clint plucked Kirra from Royce's arms and held her up over his head. "You're just absolutely crazy, aren't you?"

The baby-talk voice he used matched the kissy face he made as Kirra batted at his nose with her claws extended, and it was all just a little much for Shawn. "I'm not sure *she's* the one who's crazy," he muttered, leaning in close to Royce.

Royce chuckled. "Nah. Clint's not too bad once you get to know him."

"'Not too bad' isn't a ringing endorsement."

"I'll take it." Clint cradled Kirra against his chest, ignoring her indignant chirps. "It's not the worst thing he's said about me this week."

"You deserved that."

Clint shrugged in a deliberately nonchalant way that made Shawn wonder what Royce had said and what Clint had done to deserve it. There had to be an interesting story there, and Shawn wished he was close enough to either one of them to ask what it was.

"Maybe." Clint untangled Kirra's claw from his shirt and bopped her lightly on the nose. "I'm going to take her upstairs, let you take care of Shawn here."

"Just toss her through the door. She'll be fine on her own. She just wants you to think she's been neglected." Royce leaned down and looked straight into the kitten's eyes. "Don't you? I see through the act."

Kirra made a noise that sounded surprisingly like "nah" and twisted in Clint's arms. It looked like she was trying to burrow against him, her nose buried in the crook of his arm, but her legs were stretched out straight, pushing against his torso in a way that looked distinctly uncomfortable.

Clint just twisted her around and resettled her on her back. "Nah. I need to get to know my new boss here. You take care of the customer. I'm going to bond." He turned on his heel and marched to the back of the store, talking softly to the kitten the whole way.

Shawn watched him until he disappeared behind the door Royce and Kirra had come out of. "So, that happened."

"Yeah." Royce rubbed at the back of his neck, looking sheepish. "Sorry about that. I found Kirra abandoned by the side of the road the day after Christmas. She and her sister were just stuffed in a sack and dumped at the side of the road. My sister took the other one, but I couldn't find anyone to take her."

"Do you really want to?" Royce hadn't acted like someone who was just keeping an animal temporarily, but Shawn hardly knew him. This could be how he treated every stray that made its way into his shop.

"No." Royce dropped his hand back down to his side and smiled wryly. "I wanted to keep her from the minute I found her. She crawled out of the sack and straight into my lap, purring like mad. I don't think she knew she was supposed to be traumatized by being dumped." He laughed. "Anyway, Clint's been a big help this week. He's usually part time, but he's been here every day so I could take her to the vet and spend time getting her settled. He's a little weird, but—"

"He fits right in." Clint was a character, Shawn could tell that already, but he liked him, flirting and all. "This *is* Portland."

"Yes it is." Royce flashed a bright smile that left Shawn feeling weak in the knees, but quickly assumed a more professional expression. "So, what can I help you with? I assume you didn't come in just to see my new kitten."

"Well, I might have if I'd known about her," Shawn joked, "but no. I promised my mother I'd bring wine to New Year's Eve and I was hoping you could help me pick some out again."

"Glad to." Royce stood a little straighter, squared his shoulders, and ran his fingers through his hair. The change was subtle, but in the space of a few seconds he transformed from a slightly harried man who'd spent the morning chasing after a kitten to a suave professional who could have swept Shawn off his feet with just a few sweet words. "What would you like?"

Shawn bit back the temptation to say something raunchy and smiled. "Whatever you recommend. I was just told to bring some wine."

3

SHAWN stepped through the door of All Corked Up and blinked as he took in the people milling around. The other times he'd stopped in, he'd been the only customer, but tonight, the jingling of the chime above the door was lost in the noise of the crowd, and two unfamiliar women were standing behind the bar toward the back of the shop, chatting and pouring wine.

Clint was behind the counter at the front, and he grinned as Shawn approached. "Shawn! You're back!"

"Yeah." Shawn smiled and stepped up to the counter. "Royce mentioned tastings the last time I was in and I thought I'd stop by and see what it was all about. I didn't expect it to be this busy, though."

"Our tastings are popular." Clint typed something into the computer and frowned at the list. "Did you sign up ahead of time?"

"No. It was a last-minute decision." He glanced around again, taking in the people moving between the two rooms of the shop. Even with the second room open, the shop was almost full to capacity, with barely any room for people to move around. "Is there room? You're not sold out, are you?"

"Technically, yes." Clint shrugged and typed something into the computer. "But I can squeeze you in."

"Are you sure? I don't want to get you in trouble."

"I'll be in more trouble if I let you leave." Clint handed Shawn a wine glass and motioned toward the other room. "Royce is in there. Go hang out at his bar."

"But—"

"Go!" Clint pointed imperiously. "The boss man will fire me if I deprive him of the chance to flirt with you."

Shawn's heart did a little flip in his chest at the thought that Royce wanted to flirt with him. That didn't mean he was interested in anything more than flirting, but Clint's words gave him hope.

The other room was just as crowded as the first. It was smaller, with a counter along one wall, benches in front of the windows, and a bar in the middle of the far wall. Appetizers were set up on a table opposite the bar, and wine boxes stacked as high as Shawn's head lined the walls behind the table and next to the bar. People filled almost every bit of available space, milling about in the open center as well as in front of the bar and table, filling the room almost to capacity.

Shawn wove through the crowd, heading straight for the bar where Royce was standing next to a woman with brown skin and long dark hair pulled into a ponytail. They were both busy, smiling and laughing as they poured the wine out of the decanters and bottles set out on the table, serving a steady flow of customers with an easy rhythm that Shawn didn't particularly want to interrupt.

He hesitated in the middle of the room and wondered if he'd be able to hide in the crowd enough to slip past Clint and leave without being noticed or if Clint would spot him the minute he stepped back into the main room and order him back in here. He'd just decided the latter was more likely when Royce looked up, spotted him, and smiled wider than he had at any of the customers Shawn had watched him serve.

"Shawn!" Royce waved him over with one hand as he poured wine into a woman's cup with the other. "I didn't know you were coming!"

"It was a last-minute decision." Shawn stopped at the end of the bar, careful to stay out of the way of the people in front of it. He didn't want to cut in line, no matter how much Clint thought Royce wanted him here. "I didn't realize you'd be so busy."

"Isn't it great? This one sold out. We don't usually have this many people in January. I don't know what happened, but I'll take it. Clint let you in?"

"Yeah. I told him I'd come back when he said it was sold out, but he wouldn't let me leave. He said you'd fire him if I did."

"Damn straight I would. I've been hoping you'd come back. Wait right there, okay?" Royce turned back to the line without getting Shawn's answer and poured two glasses from the second-to-last decanter for the man standing in front of him. "This is a blend of cabernet, Syrah, and merlot from the Sonoma valley. It has a rich flavor with hints of berries, and goes really well with hard cheeses."

The man moved on, joining his companion on the benches by the window, and Royce served four more people before turning back to Shawn. "You want anything?"

"Uh." Shawn looked at the row of wines laid out on the bar. He felt like he should say no since he hadn't paid for anything when Clint handed him a glass, but he felt weird being the only person in the room not drinking something. Even Royce and the woman behind the bar had glasses they were sipping from between customers. He could always pay later, even if it meant coming back another day.

Perhaps especially if it meant coming back another day.

"What are my options?" There were eight wines out, four in bottles on ice and four in decanters, and from where Shawn was standing he could only see the labels on two of them.

"You want to just do the tasting? I recommend you go in order and start with the first white on the list, but if you want to start somewhere else, I can pour anything for you." Royce picked up Shawn's glass and rolled the stem between his fingers. "If you just want the reds, I can go through those in order too."

"I'll do the whole thing," Shawn decided. "That's the point, right? To try new things?" White wine wasn't his favorite, but it seemed silly not to at least taste it. He could always pour what he didn't like into the silver dump bucket sitting on the end of the bar.

"Absolutely." Royce handed Shawn's glass to the woman standing next to him. "Can you pour some of the Lava Cap for me, Lisa?"

"Sure." Lisa poured about an inch of pale wine into Shawn's glass and handed it back to Royce. "Here you go."

"Thanks." Royce, in turn, handed the glass to Shawn. "This is Lava Cap chardonnay. It's a California chardonnay, fruity with a little bit of tannins from being oaked. It goes well with lighter foods like white fish and it can provide a nice balance to spicy foods."

Shawn took a sip, swished the wine around in his mouth a little, and swallowed. "Huh. It's um, okay, I guess." It was drinkable, he supposed, but nothing like the wine he'd had at Christmas or New Year's Eve, and this wasn't one he'd be buying for later.

"You don't have to like it," Royce commented with a slight chuckle. "It's my least favorite out of all these."

"So why do you have it?" Shawn dumped the rest of the glass into the bucket and handed his glass back to Royce. "Shouldn't you serve wines you like?"

"If I only served wines I liked, I'd have a much smaller selection." Royce passed the glass to Lisa and asked her to fill it with the second white wine. "This tasting is staff favorites from last year, and that is Brandy's. She's one of the girls working the other bar."

"Ah." Shawn took his refilled glass back from Royce. "And whose is this?"

"Lisa's."

She smiled and nodded at Shawn but didn't say anything as another customer came up to the bar just then and asked for the third white. Shawn nodded back even though she wasn't looking at him, and took a sip. "This one's better."

Royce took a sip from his own glass, something red, though Shawn couldn't have picked out which wine it was. "I like it better too. That one's a Chablis, which is a vineyard in the Burgundy region of France. It's the chardonnay grape, same as the first one you tasted, but it's more northerly and has shallower soil, so the mineral content is higher, and they don't oak."

"It changes the flavor a lot." Shawn took another sip, swirling it around in his mouth. This wine was crisp and reminded him of fresh pears, whereas the first one he'd tasted had a flavor that was more like overly ripe peaches than anything else. "How does anyone prefer the first one to this?"

"It depends on what you're used to." Royce shrugged. "There's nothing wrong with a Californian chardonnay, and this is actually a fairly high quality one. A lot of people in the United States start off drinking California wines, and they get used to the flavor. When they get a French chardonnay, it doesn't taste right to them."

"Makes sense, I guess." Shawn drained the rest of his glass.

"I was going to suggest you try it with food," Royce said dryly. "It can change the flavor significantly."

"Oh." Disappointment wrapped around Shawn like a heavy blanket, smothering him with his need to please Royce and find out if there was a chance for this to turn into more than flirting while Shawn bought wine from Royce. He glanced at the food table, saw there weren't too many people crowded around it at the moment, and handed his glass back. "Why don't you give me a little more then, and I'll go grab something to eat?"

The pleased smile on Royce's face made Shawn's disappointment slip away like a blanket falling from his shoulders to the floor. He matched it with one of his own before he slipped across the room, dodging customers with full plates and half-empty glasses to reach the food.

The spread was surprisingly thorough. A plate with three different cheeses sat at one end of the table next to a basket of baguette slices. Next to that was a basket of tortilla chips with two bowls of salsa in front of it. On the other end of the table were three food warmers filled with things Shawn couldn't identify but that looked delicious.

"Bored with Royce already?"

"No." Shawn put the tongs back in the container holding some sort of breaded ball and turned to look at Clint. "He sent me over here to get food. Maybe he's bored with me already." He didn't really believe that, not with the signals he'd been getting all night and Clint's blatant hints, but it didn't hurt to fish for additional confirmation.

Clint snorted disbelievingly. "Impossible. He's been wondering when you were coming back for three weeks now."

"Really?" Shawn had been thinking about coming back ever since he'd stopped in the last time, but with the number of customers Royce had, he found it hard to believe Royce had been thinking about him stopping in.

"Yes." Clint put his hand on Shawn's shoulder and steered him to the side of the table. "Look, the guy has a crush on you. Thinks you're all that and a bag of chips. Thing is, he's not going to do anything about it because you're a customer and he'd rather you come in and let him flirt with you every couple of weeks than have you never come back again."

Oh. Huh. That was good news, though Shawn hadn't expected to be told quite so blatantly about Royce's feelings. He wondered if Royce knew Clint talked like this. "So, if I were to ask him out?"

"You'd better." Clint cast an exasperated glance toward Royce. "Seriously. He'll keep pining from afar forever, and I'm only going to wait so long before I take matters into my own hands."

"And do what? Set us up?"

"No." Clint looked Shawn up and down, his gaze appraising. "Look. The *only* reason I haven't tried to tap that is because the boss man called dibs. If one of you doesn't make a move soon, I'm going to make one."

Shawn stared at Clint as he tried to process that statement. It was flattering, in a way, but crude enough it was almost insulting, and he honestly wasn't sure how to feel about it. Clint wasn't unattractive—Shawn had admitted when they first met that he might have been interested if he hadn't already met Royce—but that didn't mean he wanted to have Clint pursue him if things didn't work out with Royce. It would be weird.

"I'm actually not sure how I should respond to that," he finally said in a hesitant tone, unsure how Clint would respond. "Sorry?"

Clint looked up at Shawn with a disbelieving expression on his face. "You should respond by marching over there and asking him to dinner tomorrow night," he said in a tone that clearly stated that it should have been obvious. "Get some of the cheese balls and tortilla rolls and go back over there before he thinks I'm trying to steal you away."

"You aren't?" Shawn put some of the breaded balls and crispy rolls on his plate, deliberately not looking at Clint so he wouldn't see the grin he was fighting to keep off his face.

"No. I'm trying to set you two up." Clint shoved Shawn none too gently toward the wine bar and didn't look at all repentant when he stumbled and almost dropped his food. "Now go ask him out."

It should have been easy to do with Clint's assurance that Royce was interested, but when Shawn got back to the bar, there was a line of people in front of it, and Royce was too busy pouring and explaining red wine to do more than nod and smile at Shawn when he took his place by the side of the bar again. Shawn tried to wait patiently—this was Royce's business and being busy was a good thing—but he lost a bit of confidence with every passing moment. Royce was only serving the fourth customer out of about ten when Shawn decided he needed liquid courage and took a sip of the wine Royce had waiting for him.

Absently, he took a bite of the food he'd brought over, then another sip of the wine, and was surprised to find the flavor completely different than before. It had been good, much better than the first one, but with the spiciness of the tortilla roll lingering on his tongue, it was phenomenal. "Wow."

Royce grinned at him between customers. "I told you it was better with food."

Shawn put his hand on his chest, pressing hard as though that would calm the sudden rapid beating of his heart. "I will always trust your wisdom when it comes to wine."

"As you should." Royce winked before he turned to the next customer, and Shawn gripped the bar countertop so he didn't fall on suddenly weak knees.

It was a few more minutes before the line of customers was done and Royce could devote his attention to Shawn again. By the time he did, Shawn had finished the second glass of the Chablis, and Royce refilled his glass with the third white wine. "It's a Riesling, from the Rhône Valley. It's crisp and—just a second."

The next half an hour passed in much the same way, with Royce talking to Shawn as much as he could and refilling his glass every time it got empty, but with most of his explanations cut off in the middle when another customer approached the wine bar. It wasn't until Shawn was ready for the last red wine that Royce actually got a real break as Clint stepped behind the bar.

"I got this until Jess gets a line of people ready to check out," he said, shoving Royce toward Shawn with more force than he'd used on Shawn earlier. "You two go flirt."

Royce ducked his head, but he obediently filled Shawn's glass with the last red, topped his own glass off from the same decanter, and led Shawn to the back corner of the room. "Sorry about that," he said, rubbing the back of his neck with his free hand. He looked amazing in the dim light, his face all flushed from some combination of embarrassment, alcohol, and hard work, and Shawn had trouble focusing on what he was saying rather than how he looked.

"Why?" Shawn asked when he was sure no further explanation was forthcoming. Royce clearly thought he should be sorry for something, but Shawn wasn't going to object to Clint's crudeness when it led to time essentially alone with Royce. "I thought it was nice of Clint to take over."

"Yes, but he shouldn't have said that." Royce looked down so Shawn couldn't meet his eyes. "You're a customer."

He sounded so worried about how Shawn would react to what Clint had said that Shawn decided to take all the hints the world—and Clint—had been throwing at him tonight and go for it. "A customer who would like it if you'd come to dinner with him tomorrow night."

"Yeah, but—" Royce looked up, a cautiously hopeful expression on his face. "Wait. Dinner? Where? When? Why?"

"Yes, haven't picked a place yet, seven if that works for you, and because I'm attracted to you and would like to get to know you better when you're not working," Shawn rattled off, not pausing for breath until he was done.

"Oh." Royce looked down at his wine long enough that Shawn started to doubt the information Clint had given him, but when he looked up he was smiling. "Then yes. Only, can we make it eight? I don't close the shop until seven, and we're usually busy on Saturday afternoons. I don't want to leave whoever is working alone so I can get ready."

Shawn's worry evaporated, leaving him feeling so light he thought he could fly away if he really put his mind to it. "Eight it is. I can meet you here?"

"Sounds good." Royce glanced over Shawn's shoulder and grimaced. "I'd better send Clint back to the register. You going to hang out?"

"Absolutely."

4

SHAWN tapped his fingers on the steering wheel as he tried to decide if he should park and attempt to find the outside entrance to Royce's apartment or if he should wait in the car and hope Royce came out. They hadn't planned much yesterday beyond meeting at All Corked Up at eight, and it wasn't until the drive over that Shawn had realized the store would be closed. He didn't know where they were going to meet since he couldn't go inside.

Just as the car clock flashed to 8:05—Shawn's self-imposed deadline for making a decision—Royce stepped out of the store, locked the door behind him, and looked up and down the street. His expression brightened when he noticed Shawn sitting behind the wheel of his navy-blue Prius, and he jogged over as Shawn unlocked the passenger side door.

"Sorry," he said as he climbed in. "I forgot you don't have my number. I was waiting for you to call or text."

Shawn shook his head ruefully as he pulled away from the curb. He'd really botched this "asking Royce out" thing last night, something he blamed on nerves and Clint's incessant meddling, and he was amazed how well it was all coming together. "Yeah. Sorry. I meant to ask last night, but I kept getting distracted. I didn't even realize I wouldn't be able to just walk into the store until I was halfway here."

"Don't take all the blame. I forgot to ask too. Hell, I meant to look up your number in the computer today and call, but I was busier than I expected, and Lisa had to leave early to take her son to a football game."

"We're awesome at this."

"We're managing. We'll just trade numbers when we get to the restaurant." Royce adjusted the angle of the vent. "Where are we going, anyway? I had to guess how to dress since you wouldn't tell me. I hope it's okay."

Shawn glanced over after he stopped the car at a red light. Royce was wearing jeans with dark hiking boots and a blue-and-gray-flecked sweater. It fit in perfectly in Portland, where people wore jeans just about everywhere, but Shawn still thought he looked fairly dressy. His hair was mussed in a deliberate and artful interpretation of the bedhead look that had entranced Shawn the day he'd met Clint and Kirra, but his face was freshly shaven without even a hint of a five o'clock shadow. The whole look was fantastic and went well with Shawn's choice of jeans, loafers, and a pale-gray-and-white-striped button-down shirt.

"It's perfect." Shawn instantly regretted his choice of words. Royce did look perfect, or close enough in his book anyway, but professing things like that before they'd even gotten to the restaurant on their first date probably wasn't the best way to get a second. He had to correct it before he scared Royce away. "You'll fit right in. We're going to Caffe Mingo, if that's okay."

"Of course." Royce settled back into his seat as Shawn pulled the car forward. "I love Italian. And their wine list."

"That was the primary reason I picked it," Shawn admitted. "Karen loves their wine selection, and I figured you'd prefer someplace that serves wine with dinner." Belatedly, it occurred to him that Royce might want to avoid wine since he worked with it all day, but fortunately it didn't seem to be something that made the people who worked with it all day never want to see it again. Either that, or Royce just *really* liked wine.

"I don't have to have it, but it's nice. More, ah, romantic."

"Right." Shawn parked the car and unbuckled his seat belt. "Shall we? I didn't make a reservation, but hopefully the wait won't be too long."

"After you."

Shawn led the way into the restaurant. He held the door but let Royce take it from him so he wouldn't seem overly solicitous, and greeted the hostess with a bright smile. Luck was on their side and they were seated immediately at a small table near a window that looked out over the patio. In warmer months people ate out there too, but mid-January was too cold to sit outside.

As soon as they were settled, the hostess promised their server would be with them shortly and left after handing them both menus. Shawn opened his menu and glanced over it. He only took a moment to decide that he wanted the sugo of beef braised in Chianti and espresso with penne pasta tonight. Someday, he would be more adventuresome with his food choices instead of settling on a usual at every restaurant he frequented, but tonight he was being adventurous enough. That decided, he closed his menu, set it to the side of his plate, and folded his hands as he tried to wait patiently for Royce to finish reading through. "I thought you'd eaten here before," he said after a moment when Royce was still looking at the menu and showing no signs of being close to a decision.

"I have, but it's been a while." Royce glanced up briefly, smiled, and returned his gaze to the menu. "I always read everything on a menu. There's usually something I haven't seen before even at the places I go to all the time."

That was one area they weren't compatible, but opposite ordering styles at restaurants was hardly an impediment to dating, and Shawn was perfectly capable of waiting patiently while Royce carefully read each item description. He ended up reading half the menu himself, though he didn't change his mind about what he was going to get, before Royce put down the menu. "Find something?"

"I think I'm going to get the riccia pasta with Dungeness crab. I've never had it before, but it sounds good."

Shawn read the description and had to agree. It did sound good. "Any wine? I thought I'd let you pick the bottle. You'll do better than I would."

Royce laughed as he looked over the wine list. "I should have you pick so you can learn."

"How about you pick and tell me why?" He'd ruin the date by picking the worst possible bottle if he just jumped right in. "I'll pick once I know more."

"Fair enough." Royce nodded his agreement. "I'm going to hold you to that, though, so don't think you're getting out of it."

Shawn's heart leaped. Royce hadn't balked at the implication they would have more dates, and, better yet, he'd agreed with it. It was still early in the date, with plenty of time left for something to go wrong, but he was taking that as a sign of a successful evening. "I wouldn't dream of it."

"Good. Now, what are you having?" Royce opened his menu again and set it in the table so he could look at it while he read the wine list. "I need to match the wine to both our entrees."

"The sugo of beef braised in Chianti and espresso with penne pasta."

Royce took a moment to skim the description then ran his finger down the list of wines. A little more than two-thirds of the way through the reds, he stopped and tapped the page twice. "This one, I think." He laid the list on the table so Shawn could see the wine he'd chosen. "Isole e Olena Chianti Classico. It's heavy enough it will complement the meat in your dish, but not so heavy it will overwhelm the seafood in mine. It's smooth and has good flavor that will also complement a lot of desserts."

"Works for me." Shawn peered at the wine list. It was also a moderately priced bottle, not so expensive it should be reserved for a special occasion, but not the cheapest thing on the menu either. If the flavor lived up to Royce's assessment—and Shawn had no reason to doubt it would—it was an excellent choice. "How do you remember all that about each kind of wine anyway?"

"I drink a lot." Royce chuckled. "It sounds bad, but it's part of the job. I sample each wine we have out to taste so I can talk about it, and I visit a lot of vineyards to try their wine too."

"A little bit of a lot of different wines, then?"

"Yeah. Two to four sips of whatever I'm tasting to be sure I get the real flavor and a glass or two with or after dinner." Royce shrugged. "It looks like a lot more than it actually is. Most days, I get a whole lot of variety, but not a lot of actual alcohol."

"Best way to do it."

"Probably." Royce smiled slyly. "Better than the other way around, anyway."

"Yeah." The other way around was Shawn's experience, though he thought Royce's sounded much better. He was searching for a way to say that without sounding pathetic when the waitress arrived in a flurry of napkins and water glasses.

"I am *so* sorry," she said in a breathless voice as she pushed her glasses up her nose. "I was on my break and no one told me I had someone new sitting in my section."

"It's all right," Shawn said, waving off her concern. "Things happen."

"Thanks." She visibly relaxed for a moment before perking up and beaming at them with the brightest smile Shawn had ever seen on a server. "Well, I'm Carrie. Did I give you two enough time to pick what you want to eat, or do I need to get lost for a few more minutes? I'd be happy to extend my break if you need it."

"I think we're good," Shawn said with a suppressed laugh.

"If you're sure." She pulled a pen and pad out of her apron pocket. "Whenever you're ready."

Royce gave her his order first, including the wine, then Shawn ordered his dish and handed over their menus. Carrie thanked them and left after promising to return with their wine. When she was gone, Shawn sat back in his chair and looked at Royce. "So."

"So," Royce echoed, clearly feeling—like Shawn did—that the conversation had reached a natural stopping point just before Carrie showed up. "What now?"

"Well, we could keep talking about wine, since I'm sure you have a wealth of knowledge on the subject," Shawn suggested, though that really wasn't what he wanted to do. Royce could teach him a lot about wine, he was sure, and he wanted to learn at least some of it eventually, but that wasn't part of his preferred agenda for tonight. "Or—"

"Or you could tell me about *your* hobbies," Royce suggested, looking just as thrilled about the idea of discussing wine as Shawn was.

Shawn rarely told people about his hobby, but at the moment he wanted to tell Royce, so he spit out the words before he could stop himself. "I'm an artist. Well, sort of," he corrected, slowing down a little now that the secret was out of the bag. "I draw for fun. Paint too, a little, but only when the weather is nice so I can do it outside."

"Sounds like you're more than 'sort of' an artist to me."

"I don't make any money from it, though, and a lot of it isn't original stuff either. I do a lot of fan art—video game and TV characters, that sort of thing."

Royce raised an eyebrow. "So? You're the one drawing it or painting it, right? That makes you an artist." He leaned in, resting his forearms on the edge of the table. "Lots of people practice by copying other artists' work, and you don't have to make money on something to take the title. Artists are people who make art. Period."

"Tell my mother that, would you?" Shawn muttered, thinking of the way his mother nagged him about the time she thought he wasted on his art. It didn't matter what he drew or painted. If he wasn't making money on it, his mother didn't believe it was worth the effort he put in.

"She's not a fan, huh?"

"She just thinks I could better spend my time working on something that pays, or at least something *she* thinks is relaxing. To her, drawing and painting are work, and work deserves pay."

Royce winced sympathetically. "Ouch. I can see her point, I guess, about work deserving pay, but you obviously don't think what you do is work. Even I can tell that."

"I know she just wants what's best for me, but sometimes she drives me nuts." Shawn let out a little huff of annoyance. He hadn't meant to vent at Royce, but somehow discussing his art almost always led him to talking about his mother's less than stellar opinion of it. It usually took a little longer than this to bring her around in the conversation, but he was unusually relaxed around Royce. "Sorry. You didn't come here to listen to me bitch about my mother."

"It's fine." Royce smiled in a way that made Shawn believe he meant it. "I get it. My mother does the same thing. You should have heard her when I opened All Corked Up."

"She doesn't like it?" That was difficult to imagine. From what Shawn could tell, All Corked Up was a successful business, one any mother would be proud of her son for owning and running.

"She likes it now. But when I started it, she was worried that I would lose all the money I'd invested. And to be fair, it was a lot. I had to renovate the building and buy the wine before I could sell it. Enough wine to open a wine store doesn't come cheaply."

"Wait. You *started* the shop?" Shawn didn't know why—he hadn't heard anything either way—but he had assumed Royce had bought All Corked Up from someone. It still would have been a sizeable investment, but at least it would have been a presumably solid one with a history of successful sales behind it. Shawn could hardly imagine the risk Royce had taken starting from scratch.

"Yep." Royce looked justifiably proud. "I was in school studying for a law degree I didn't want when my grandfather died and left me a pretty big inheritance. Wine was one passion we shared, and I decided the best way to honor him was to use the money for something that would let me share that passion with other people."

"Wow." Shawn tried not to think about how out of his league Royce suddenly seemed. Shawn barely had the courage to share his art with people and selling it wasn't something he'd ever managed to consider despite his mother's nagging. He had a good job, but he was just a manager at the restaurant. A manager with dreams of more, true, but dreams didn't compare to what Royce had already done. "Why didn't you buy a shop, then? Your mother would have been happier."

"I thought about it, but it didn't seem right. Grandpa never did things the easy way. Besides, starting it let me pick the name, what we stocked, everything. It's completely my baby. Well, mine and Grandpa's. The name is his."

"It is? How?"

"He used to say he was all corked up when he'd had enough to drink for the night." Royce gaze got distant as he lost himself in the memory. "We'd go to various shops to taste wine. When he was ready to leave, he'd say 'Royce, I'm all corked up, how 'bout you?' and that's when we'd head home. I never knew what his criteria was—some nights he'd just have a couple glasses and some nights he'd have practically a whole bottle—but he always said that when he'd reached his limit."

"Wow. That's... incredible." Shawn wished his vocabulary wasn't failing him at the moment, but it was all he could do not to stare at Royce with his mouth hanging open in shock. Even if he managed to achieve his dream someday, he wouldn't have a story like that to share.

"I guess." Royce looked less than thrilled with the praise.

"You guess?" Shawn didn't bother to hide his incredulity. "You're doing what you love and honoring your grandfather. Most people only dream of being able to achieve that. And you did it all by, what, thirty?" He had no idea how long All Corked Up had been open other than that it was relatively well-established, but he figured Royce was around his age. He couldn't have been much older than thirty when he opened the store unless Shawn was drastically wrong about his age.

"By thirty-three, but close enough," Royce corrected. "We'll have been open eight years in May."

"Wow." Shawn really needed to come up with another word to express his astonishment or Royce was going to think he was an idiot. "When I was thirty-three, I was… doing the exact same thing I'm doing now, actually." It had seemed awesome at the time, and he was usually happy with his life and his plans for the future, but right now he felt like a failure compared to Royce.

"What is that, anyway? I don't think you ever told me."

"I'm the day-shift manager at Delicto. It's a little pub down on Northwest Flanders. Nothing huge, but it keeps me busy, and I'm hoping to buy it when the owner is ready to retire."

"Any idea when that will be?"

"Sometime in the next year, I hope. I'm almost forty and I'm not sure my mother will forgive me if I make it past that without really making something of myself." He rolled his eyes as he said the last words, hearing his mother's voice in his head.

"Manager *is* making something of yourself."

"Yeah, well, not to my mother. She wants the best for her children."

Royce shared a sympathetic smile. "All mothers do. I'm sure it'll be fine."

Shawn wished he could have Royce's confidence, but he couldn't dwell on it now. "Eventually. I just might end up at your shop bitching and moaning if things don't go according to plan."

"All bitching and moaning is to be directed at Clint, but I'll happily keep you in wine while you wallow."

"Shouldn't you take complaints as the owner?"

"Complaints about the store or the wine we sell, sure. Complaints about life outside the store are Clint's job. Or Lisa's if he's not in."

Shawn chuckled. "Seems like an awful lot to put on them."

"I pay well!"

"Of course you do." Shawn chuckled and sat back in his seat, suddenly feeling more relaxed. Royce laughed too, and by the time Carrie returned with their food, Shawn had forgotten why he'd ever been nervous.

5

SHAWN'S good mood lasted until he arrived at work Sunday morning and found his boss, Henry Reid, sitting in his car outside the restaurant waiting for him. The consensus among the staff at Delicto was the earlier Henry showed up, the worse a day was going to be, and this was the earliest Shawn had ever seen him. Even the day after they'd been robbed he hadn't shown up until ten thirty to talk to the police. Shawn couldn't imagine what would have him here at nine fifteen.

He ran through a few worst-case scenarios in his head as he parked his Prius next to Henry's old Lincoln Town Car, but he was as clueless when he climbed out as when he'd first pulled into the lot. With trepidation, he walked around to the driver's side of the Lincoln. "Henry."

"Shawn." Henry climbed laboriously out of his car.

Shawn clasped his hands behind his back so he wouldn't be tempted to help. Henry was eighty-three, frail, and looked as though he couldn't manage more than two steps without assistance, but he vehemently rejected every offer he received. Shawn had tried to help him into the car once, back when he'd first started serving here, and it had gotten him assigned to dish duty for three weeks. Every person who tried to help since had gotten a similar response, and only one person had dared try twice. She no longer worked at Delicto, though she'd left before Shawn had been promoted to manager and he had no idea if she'd quit or had been let go. The rumor mill said the latter, and Shawn had long since decided he didn't want to know if it was true.

"Inside." Henry pushed his car door shut, grunting with the effort, and shuffled toward the building.

Shawn glanced at the car, decided it would be more trouble than it was worth to double-check the door, and followed along, keeping his steps small so he didn't overtake his boss before they got inside. He managed to open the outside door for Henry by virtue of having his building key out and ready, but Henry insisted on opening the second heavy door all by himself and only let Shawn take it when the opening was wide enough to slip through.

It was extreme behavior even from Henry, who took being able to do things despite his frail body as a point of pride, and it made an uneasy feeling settle in the pit of Shawn's stomach. By the time they reached the small room in the back that served as both a breakroom and a meeting room, Shawn's good mood from last night had completely been replaced by worry.

"I heard you had a date last night." Henry sat in the most comfortable chair at the old table that occupied most of the space in the small room and motioned for Shawn to take the seat across from him.

The chair there was the worst one in the room, a rickety thing that looked as though it would fall apart if Shawn sat on it for long, so he swapped it with the one next to it and took a seat. "I did." He wasn't sure how Henry had heard or what business of his it was, but he wasn't going to lie about the best night he'd had in quite some time.

Henry sneered. "With a man."

Henry was a product of his time, a man who still believed that gay relationships should be illegal. Shawn had known since his then-boyfriend had stopped by to congratulate him his first night as manager, but he'd long since decided to ignore it. He couldn't change Henry's mind, but he didn't think he needed to. Aside from making his position on the whole issue clear, Henry hadn't said or done anything to hurt Shawn, and he was generally a decent boss. With the money he made as the day-shift manager and the possibility he'd be able to buy the restaurant when Henry retired, Shawn had decided it was worth it to stay.

"Yes. That's who I usually go on dates with." This was hardly the first date Shawn had been on since the night he'd discovered Henry didn't approve, and it wouldn't be the last. For the first two years he'd been manager, he'd been in a long-term relationship that had only ended because his boyfriend had moved to New York City to pursue a job opportunity there and Shawn hadn't been interested in moving or in having a long-distance relationship. Royce was the first guy he'd been genuinely interested in since his relationship with Tom had ended, but he'd hardly been celibate in the intervening three years.

The look on Henry's face would have made his feelings on the matter clear even if Shawn hadn't known them. "I thought you wanted to buy this place."

Shawn blinked as he tried to process the apparent change of subject. "I'd like to, yes." He had close to enough money saved up for a decent down payment, and if Henry waited another nine to twelve months to retire, Shawn would easily be able to get a loan for the fair market value. He had the experience needed to convince the bank he could make it work, too, as long as the timing was right. "Why?"

"I'm not selling to a fag."

Shawn barely managed not to wince at the term. "I've been gay the entire time I've worked here, Henry," he said in a carefully controlled voice. He hadn't thought it would matter so long as he kept his dates away from the restaurant and didn't shove his relationships in Henry's face, and he'd long accepted the need to do that. "You know that. You were willing to sell to me when we talked about it last week."

"Last week you weren't flaunting your unnatural activities." Henry looked at the space just to the side of Shawn's head. "I can't sell my business to someone who goes around blatantly corrupting today's youth like that. I'd lose people's respect. You'd lose their business. What would happen to everyone who works here? People are depending on me to keep this place open."

There were homophobic people in Portland—no place was truly free of them—but most people were either very accepting or just didn't care. Any customers who would be driven away by Shawn being gay had probably already left, as had any employees, because he hadn't hidden it from anyone. He would never convince Henry of that, though.

"I think most people already know I'm gay, Henry." He looked straight at Henry, ignoring the way Henry was refusing to look at him, and willed himself to stay calm. It wasn't supposed to happen this way, especially not now, when he was so close to being able to buy the place and had finally found someone he was interested in.

"I hope not. I asked you not to flaunt that around here."

"I don't flaunt anything. I just don't lie about it." It was hard enough when the servers and bartenders had their girlfriends and boyfriends stop by and he didn't dare invite the person he was dating. He had drawn the line at not saying anything when dates or significant others came up in conversation. "I haven't brought any of my dates here since my first night as manager. You can't ask me to do anything else."

"I don't have to sell to you, though." Henry sighed, leaned back in his chair, and looked Shawn in the eyes for the first time. "I like you, Shawn, despite your perversion, and I'd like to be able to sell this restaurant to you. I want to retire soon, and you've been with me the longest. You know your stuff and you have the skills to make it work."

It sounded good, but Shawn knew there was more to it than that. "But?"

"But I can't sell to you if you're flaunting what you are. I'm sorry." He sounded genuinely regretful, which made the whole thing worse. Henry didn't hate him because he was gay; Shawn knew that. Henry genuinely thought there was something wrong with him, that he was sick somehow, and that there had to be something Shawn could do to fix it. In Henry's mind, it was a good thing to employ someone with that kind of illness—it showed what a thoughtful person he was and how much he cared. Obviously, it was quite another thing to sell his business to Shawn or anyone else who flaunted their so-called illness.

"Going on a date is hardly flaunting, Henry." Shawn fought to keep his voice even by reminding himself there was more at stake here than his pride. "I had dinner."

"You had dinner with another *man*."

"Who could have been a friend just as easily as a date." Shawn honestly wasn't sure what had tipped Henry off. He'd had a wonderful time with Royce, but they hadn't even kissed until he'd dropped Royce off. No casual observer should have been able to tell they were anything other than two friends enjoying dinner together.

Then again, whoever had tipped Henry off obviously knew him, and maybe there had been tells that someone who knew him well could notice. He really wanted to ask who it was—he couldn't think of anyone he knew well who would talk to Henry about anything other than work—but in the end it didn't matter. He had been on a date, and he wasn't going to deny it, no matter what Henry wanted him to do.

"You have two choices here, Shawn," Henry said softly. "You can keep doing things just as you have been and I'll sell this place to you when I retire, or you can stop fighting your illness and keep seeing this guy and I won't. I'm not going to fire you, Shawn, not unless you bring him here and disrupt things, but I can't sell to you if you give in like this. I need to be sure the restaurant will be in good hands."

Shawn clenched his hands under the table and tried to remind himself Henry was a product of his time, nothing more. "It will be in good hands."

"I need to be able to trust that, Shawn." Henry leaned forward, resting one hand on the table as he met Shawn's gaze. "Is this *man* really worth giving up everything you've worked for?"

That was the rub. Shawn liked Royce—*really* liked Royce—but he'd seen the guy a grand total of four times. They weren't exactly at Happily Ever After yet. "I don't know."

"Think about it." Henry stood, using the table to lever himself up, and for once Shawn didn't have to fight the urge to help him. "I want what's best for you and the restaurant, Shawn. I hope you can see that."

Shawn nodded once but otherwise held his body perfectly still, his muscles tight, gripping the underside of the table. He didn't speak, didn't trust himself to speak, and didn't let himself move beyond the terse bob of his head until Henry was out of the room. The moment the door closed, he slumped, his breath leaving in a sharp burst of air as the tension drained from his muscles. "Fuck."

He stared at the ceiling for a minute, contemplating the uncovered beams. The third one from the door had a crack in it, and the fifth was dented in several places, a result of a wild New Year's Eve several years earlier. The one closest to the far wall had holes in the bottom where hooks had been pulled out. When Shawn had started here, a bar had hung there for people to put their coats on or hang umbrellas from, but just before Shawn was promoted it was taken down, replaced by a small refrigerator and cubbies. The refrigerator was nice, since they weren't allowed to keep personal food in the kitchen, but the cubbies didn't work nearly as well as the makeshift coat rack had, particularly on rainy days.

Shawn had thought about putting the coat rack back up when he bought the place, though maybe a shorter version, so he could keep the cubbies for bags and other personal belongings. It was just one of many things he'd thought about changing. The idea that he wouldn't get the chance to implement any of them didn't sit well, but neither did the idea of giving up on his burgeoning relationship with Royce just to satisfy Henry's bigotry. There was something special there, he could feel it. He just wasn't sure it was enough to give up his dream for.

He sat there, contemplating the yellowing paint on the walls and the dust collecting in the corners and on top of the cubbies until his phone beeped at him, reminding him he had a restaurant to open. The alert was supposed to be a reminder to unlock the back door, so his opening kitchen staff could get in, but today it served the dual purpose of also reminding him he needed to set up the break schedule, do inventory, and take care of the rest of his opening duties. He should be just about done and he hadn't even started.

Shawn pinched the bridge of his nose and sighed as he tried to get his head back into the game. He had to think about what Henry had told him, but now wasn't the time, and this probably wasn't the place. It was hard to separate himself from his desire to own Delicto while he was here. He needed distance and time, but he wasn't going to get either until his shift was over, so he tried to push it out of his mind and went to unlock the door. He didn't have to make the decision just yet.

6

BY THE time Shawn got home, he wasn't sure he ever wanted to *see* Delicto again, much less buy the place. His foul mood had carried over into everything he'd done, turning minor annoyances into genuine problems and making genuine problems seem like insurmountable obstacles. Even things he could usually count on working properly had malfunctioned, and he'd come closer than he ever had before to yelling at the staff.

The result was that he was home early, kicked out by Marcie, the closing manager, within a half hour of her arrival. They were both supposed to work the start of dinner, with Shawn leaving as soon as things started to calm down, but tonight Marcie had insisted things would go better without him there. She was probably right, but it meant Shawn was home earlier than he'd planned, no decision made and no real excuse not to call Royce as he'd promised to do last night.

Shawn ate the dinner he brought home first so he could put it off as long as possible, but soon he was sitting on his couch, a beer in one hand and his phone in the other. He pulled Royce's contact information up on the screen but hesitated with his thumb hovering over the call button, wondering if it would be better just not to call. He could lie the next time he saw Royce if he decided he wanted to pursue this, tell him he got stuck late at work and had fallen asleep as soon as he got home. If he decided this wasn't worth pursuing, he could use it to drive Royce away and make the break between them as sharp as possible. Either way, he wouldn't have to talk to Royce tonight, wouldn't have to explain how his day had gone to hell in a handbasket before it had really started, and wouldn't have to think about making a decision just yet.

It was the best thing to do, but as Shawn was exiting out of the contact screen, his phone rang, and the gesture that would have closed the contact answered the call. He lifted it to his ear with a muttered curse. "Hello?"

"Shawn!" Royce sounded surprised. "I thought you'd still be at work."

"Then why'd you call?" The words were out of Shawn's mouth before he could stop them.

"I thought I'd leave a message…." Royce sounded uncertain now. "I had a few minutes and I kept thinking about last night, so I thought I'd call. Sorry?"

It was clear Royce didn't know what he was apologizing for, and that grated. Intellectually, Shawn was aware there was no way for Royce to know he would be in a bad mood, much less why, but Shawn wasn't in the mood for logic. "It's fine," he said shortly, not bothering to hide his annoyance.

"Okay…." Royce drew out the word. "Do you want me to call back later?"

"No." Shawn sighed and reminded himself he hadn't decided to give up on this yet. "I had a bad day. I'm sorry. I shouldn't have taken it out on you."

"Is there anything I can do?"

Royce's concern tore at Shawn. This would be easier if things hadn't gone so well last night, if he hadn't been attracted to Royce from the first moment he walked into his shop. He didn't need Royce to be understanding right now and make it even worse. "Not unless you can make my boss less of a homophobe."

"Ouch. I really can't, sorry." Royce sounded like he genuinely regretted it. "I can let you vent at me, though, and remind you that you'll be the boss in a year or so when you buy it from him."

"I can't buy it if he refuses to sell."

"Why would he do that? I thought you said you'd talked to him about buying the place."

"I have."

"So what changed his mind?"

Shawn really didn't want to get into this, but there wasn't a graceful way to change the subject. He could either put Royce off and make things tense between them until he made a decision or get it out in the open now. He'd always preferred to rip Band-Aids off instead of pulling them slowly, and this was no different. "Someone saw us at dinner last night and told Henry."

"Henry's your boss?"

"Yeah."

"Okay. Your boss knows we went on a date. What does that have to do with you buying the restaurant?"

"Because Henry won't sell to me if I 'flaunt my perversion'." Shawn rolled his eyes, knowing his tone conveyed the expression even though Royce couldn't see him. "I can either stop dating or give up on the idea of buying the place."

"You don't think you'll be able to change his mind?"

"He's eighty-three years old. He thinks being gay is an illness and if I'm so overcome by it that I'm dating another man, he can't trust that I'll take care of the restaurant."

"Oh." Royce was quiet for a moment. "What are you going to do?"

"I don't know." As he said it, Shawn realized he did know. He just didn't want to tell Royce yet.

"You could always buy a different restaurant," Royce suggested softly. "It wouldn't be Delicto, but I bet there are other restaurant owners in Portland willing to sell."

That clinched Shawn's decision. "I don't want to own a different restaurant. I want to own *Delicto*." Shawn fought to keep his voice steady. "I've been saving for Delicto. I've been planning for Delicto. I can't just drop everything I've worked toward for four years because of one nice date."

"So you've decided, then," Royce said softly. He almost sounded hurt, but Shawn didn't know him well enough to make that call and couldn't let himself get there. "You're going to give up on what seems like a pretty good thing so far because your boss is a bigot."

"No. I'm putting the dream I've worked toward for years first. If you can't respect that, there probably wasn't much chance for things to go far between us anyway."

"I respect your dream, Shawn. I can't respect you letting other people dictate how to achieve it. You're not going to be satisfied if you take the easy way. Trust me."

"Why? Because *you* did things the hard way?"

"Yes. I'm speaking from experience here."

Shawn snorted. It wasn't the same thing at all. "No. You got money from your grandfather that let you buy exactly what you wanted. I've had to save, and what I want is Delicto. Henry passed up another offer last year because he knew I was close to being able to afford it. I like you, Royce, I do, but I can't just walk away from that because we had one good date and a few more good conversations." He slumped on the couch and took a pull of his beer, feeling drained but confident he'd made the right choice. "I'm sorry."

"Me too. I think we could have had something." The phone crackled and rustled as Royce took a deep breath. "I guess I'll see you around."

"Yeah. See ya."

ROYCE stared at his phone for several minutes after Shawn disconnected the call, wondering what, exactly, had just happened. Last night had been great from the moment Shawn had picked him up to the good-night kiss, and Royce didn't understand how it had gone so wrong so fast. The only thing he'd been able to focus on all day was what he would say when it was finally late enough to call. The conversation hadn't gone anywhere close to the way he'd imagined it, though, and now he wished he'd put it off for a few more hours.

A soft bump against his leg interrupted his wallowing, and he looked down to see Kirra peering up at him with wide eyes. "Mrrp?"

"Hey, girl." He smiled sadly as he reached down to stroke her back. She jumped into his lap instead and purred loudly as she kneaded at his thigh.

Royce shook his head and ran one hand along her silky fur. "Do you need attention? Is Puck hiding from you again?" His older cat had been remarkably tolerant of Kirra since Royce had brought her home, but Puck was nine and starting to get lazy. Sometimes Kirra's energy was too much for him.

Sometimes her energy was too much for Royce, too, but at the moment she seemed to realize he needed comfort. She settled down on his lap like it was her rightful place and started rolling around, nuzzling him. Every few seconds, she'd stand, turn around, and flop back down in a slightly different position, purring the whole time and rubbing her face against his hand as he tried to pet her.

"This would be easier if you settled down," he said after a while, but Kirra's only response was to start gnawing gently on one of his fingers. He pulled his hand away with a hiss as her sharp teeth dug into his skin. "Stop that!"

Kirra chirped, jumped off his lap, and pranced over to the door at the top of the stairs. She pawed at it a few times and, when that didn't get Royce to open the door, she looked back at him and cried. The pitiful mewls perfectly matched the way he felt at the moment, but her problems were much more fixable than his.

"You're not going to be allowed downstairs if I add a restaurant, you know." Kirra just looked at him, clearly expecting that he would continue to cave to her every whim, and with good reason. He hadn't managed to say no to her soft chirps and wide eyes since bringing her home a month ago. "All right. Fine." He sighed as he pulled open the door. "I suppose you want me to open the one at the bottom too."

Kirra slipped through as soon as the door was open wide enough and reached the second door at the bottom of the stairs before Royce finished the sentence. As he started down, resigned to the idea that he was going back to the shop at least long enough to make sure Clint and Lisa were okay with Kirra down there, she stood on her back legs and pawed at the door, making it rattle in place.

"Kirra!" Royce picked up his pace, slapping his bare feet against the wooden stairs, one footfall for every two bangs of the door. "Patience!"

The door opened just before Royce reached the bottom stair, and Kirra darted through Clint's legs with a happy chirp. "Crazy cat," he said fondly, shaking his head as he stepped back to close the door. He froze when his gaze landed on Royce. "Boss. Didn't realize you were coming back down."

"Wasn't going to, but...." Royce shrugged and gestured vaguely in the direction Kirra had run.

Clint understood immediately. "She's a handful. I'll keep her down here for the rest of the day if you want to head back upstairs. I wouldn't want you to miss Shawn's call."

The hurt and confusion Royce had managed to push away for a few moments crashed down on him. "He won't call."

"But—" Clint broke off and looked at Royce shrewdly. "What happened? I thought you both had a good time last night?"

"Not good enough, apparently." Royce paused and ran his hand over his face as he tried to calm down some. Clint didn't deserve his ire, and if he lashed out now, he'd regret it later. "Sorry. We both had a good time, but Shawn's boss is an asshole, so we can't go out again."

"I don't see the correlation."

"Neither do I." Royce fought to keep his voice level, but failed.

Clint stepped back into the shop without letting go of the door handle and looked at the front counter. "Hey, Lisa! Will you be okay alone for a few minutes? Boss man needs me upstairs." She shouted back an affirmation, and before Royce could protest that he didn't need Clint anywhere but the shop, Clint stepped into the stairwell and shut the door. "Okay. Details," he said, pushing Royce up the stairs. He was stronger than Royce despite his shorter stature and left Royce with only two options: move or fall.

Royce held off until he got upstairs and sat back down in the same place he'd been when he called Shawn. He realized that the moment his legs hit the couch cushion but squashed the irrational desire to move. One spot on the couch wasn't more cursed than any other, and Clint already seemed to think he'd half lost his mind. He wouldn't add to the delusion by randomly deciding he couldn't sit on half his couch. "Shawn answered when I called."

"I gathered that much." Clint sat in the chair next to the couch and crossed his legs as Puck wandered into the room. The cat ignored him in favor of investigating his food bowl, and Clint directed his attention back to Royce. "What did he say? Besides that his boss is an asshole, that is."

"Pretty much just that." Royce slumped back on the couch and looked at his hands as he tried to decide how much he wanted to tell Clint. Their relationship was more friends than boss and employee, but Royce wasn't sure he wanted to get into this now. On the other hand, Clint had been instrumental in setting up the date, and it wasn't as though Royce had anyone else to talk to, unless he wanted to tell his mother about yet another failed attempt at a relationship. "He wants to buy the restaurant he works in when his boss retires, but the guy said he won't sell to Shawn if he's publicly dating another man."

"Ouch." Clint winced. "Can he do that?"

"Apparently." Royce didn't look up. "He's not firing or demoting Shawn, just saying he won't sell. If they don't have a signed contract, he can refuse to sell for whatever reason he wants."

"And Shawn doesn't have a contract?"

"I assume not." Royce didn't know, but at this point it didn't matter. Shawn had made up his mind. "It would be a little harder for his boss to screw him over if he did."

"True." Clint frowned. "That blows."

"That's one word for it." Personally, Royce preferred something stronger, but he didn't want to end the day by cursing at his best employee.

"Yeah." Clint leaned forward, rested his elbows on his knees with his hands dangling, and looked straight at Royce. "What did you say when he told you?"

Royce scowled at the memory. He didn't want to think about the conversation, but he recognized the look on Clint's face. He wasn't going to be left alone until he did. "I asked him if he could change his boss's mind, and when he said he couldn't, I said he could just buy another restaurant."

Clint groaned and let his head drop so his chin was touching his chest. "Really?"

"It's just a restaurant."

"It's the restaurant he saved for." Clint looked like he couldn't believe he was having this conversation. "How do you not get that? It's his dream. You know about chasing dreams."

"I told him that," Royce protested. "He said it was different. Said I didn't get it because I inherited the money to open this place." The jab had hurt almost as much as Shawn's refusal to stand up to his boss. No, Royce hadn't had to save for years to buy All Corked Up, but he'd put a lot of time into the store and given up on a lot of other things as he'd fought to make his dream work. Contrary to Shawn's belief, Royce did understand compromise and sacrifice for a dream. That was why his closest friend was also his employee and he only saw his family on the holidays. He hadn't wanted to give up his social life because of the store, and he hated that he'd finally started to find one again only to have it cut short because Shawn's dream was getting in the way. There had to be a way for them to follow their dreams and see where this spark between them went, but they'd never know if Shawn was too cowardly to try.

"It is different." Clint shot a warning look at Royce before he could interrupt. "Look, I know you've given up a lot to turn this place into what it is, and I respect that. Shawn respects that. But you built this place yourself because you couldn't find what you wanted. Shawn did find what he wants, and you have to respect that too. Telling him to buy another restaurant would be like… like telling you to open a different kind of store."

Royce didn't believe it was quite on that level, but Clint was clearly on Shawn's side, so there was no point in arguing. "Fine. I shouldn't have said that. I'll apologize if I see him again."

"Or you could call him," Clint pointed out blandly. "He might be willing to give you another shot if you do."

"You forget—his boss won't let him if he wants to buy the restaurant."

"You said his boss didn't want him publicly dating. You could be discreet." Clint fought a smile. "Probably."

Royce rolled his eyes. "I'm perfectly capable of being discreet. That doesn't mean Shawn will want to."

Clint stood and looked pointedly at Royce. "You won't know until you ask, will you?" He walked toward the door, paused to stroke Puck's back once as he passed, and stopped at the top of the stairs. "Think about it. I'm going back to work."

Royce waited until he heard the door close behind Clint, then sighed and stood. There was office work he could do until closing and then there was some television he wanted to watch. It wasn't how he'd planned to spend the evening, but it would be better than sitting on his couch moping. He'd think about what Clint had said later. Clint wouldn't let him get away with anything else, but he could put it off for a little while, give Shawn time to think as well, and call when his head was on straight. Until then, it was best to keep his mind busy, and paperwork followed by mindless television was perfect for that. In an hour, he wouldn't be thinking about Shawn at all.

7

THREE days later, Royce still hadn't managed to stop replaying his conversation with Shawn, wondering how it could have gone differently. It wasn't so bad that he couldn't focus on anything else, but unless he was actively engaged in something that kept his mind occupied, he thought about what Shawn had said, and what Clint had said, and tried to twist things around in his mind until the conversation ended differently. He never quite managed the result he wanted because he didn't know how Shawn would react to the changed flow, but he had done a lot of the store's paperwork trying not to think about it.

He had just finished buying enough presents to give his niece and nephew on their next three birthdays when Clint rapped on the doorframe leaned into the office. "Hey, boss, can you—Why did you just buy a six-foot-tall stuffed giraffe?"

"For Ella. I bought a giant hippo for Kyler."

"You bought your niece and nephew giant stuffed animals." Clint shook his head as if to clear it as he stepped into the room. "Why?"

"They'll like them!" Royce didn't mention the Lego sets, books, art supplies, clothes, dolls, and trains he'd also bought. "I thought they'd make good birthday presents."

"Kyler's birthday is in April and Ella's in September," Clint said flatly. "It's the end of January."

He had a valid point, but anything that shipped fast enough would provide another distraction while Royce tried to figure out where to keep it for the next several months. "I know."

"So why are you shopping now? I know you usually go overboard with their presents, but this is ridiculously early, especially for Ella. It's almost like—Oh." Clint looked at Royce shrewdly and the tiny spark of hope Royce had that he'd be able to fool Clint flickered and died. Clint was smarter than he let on and it was easy to forget sometimes. "You still haven't called Shawn, have you?"

It was amazing how Clint could make Royce feel like a chastised child with just a look. He fought against the urge to look down and forced himself to meet Clint's gaze. "No."

Clint leaned against the desk. "Why not?"

Royce didn't have a good answer for that. He'd thought about it several times while trying to rewrite the conversation in his head, but it had always been too late or too early or he'd upset himself too much and he'd never picked up the phone. "Haven't gotten around to it," he said, trying to sound nonchalant. "I've been busy."

"You've been making yourself busy, you mean. If you have time to shop for stuffed animals, you have time to call Shawn." Clint picked Royce's phone up and handed it to him. "Go on."

Royce put the phone back down. He needed to call or forget all about Shawn, he knew that, but he wasn't going to do either with Clint looming over him. "Later."

"Now." Clint nudged the phone back toward Royce. "Before you chicken out."

"I'm not chickening out. Honest."

Clint didn't look like he believed Royce and, honestly, Royce couldn't blame him. It did look like he was trying to avoid making the call, and in a way, he was. He had to be sure he actually wanted to make it before he picked up the phone.

"Sure looks like you are." Clint hopped up to sit on Royce's desk. "Do you need me to tell you you're an idiot, or do you need another heart-to-heart? I can do either, though I have to tell you, heart-to-hearts are not in my job description. I might need a raise for this."

"Yes, they are," Royce countered with a smirk. "They're 'other duties as assigned by management'. I'm management."

Clint snorted. "I don't think that phrase means what you think it means."

"It means whatever I want it to. That's the perk of being the boss. I get to pick these things."

"Yeah, well, pick Brandy or Lisa the next time you need a heart-to-heart. Brandy loves gossip."

Royce grimaced at the idea of sharing his personal life with his other employees. He liked Brandy, Lisa, and Jess on both personal and professional levels, but he wasn't friends with them like he was with Clint. Clint had been Royce's first employee, and they'd become true friends in those early days, before Royce could afford to employ anyone else. He'd barely been able to pay Clint some months, but Clint had stuck with him through it all and they'd bonded during long days and late nights when Royce's personal life had fallen apart thanks to the time he had to spend on the shop. Without Clint, Royce doubted he would have made it through the first year he owned All Corked Up.

Clint had earned the right to pry in Royce's personal life and granted Royce the same right in return. The others hadn't.

"Yeah, no," Royce said, vetoing Clint's idea. "One of the other perks of being the boss is that I get to pick who I assign jobs to. You're the lucky winner on this one."

"Fantastic," Clint said, his voice dripping with sarcasm. "I get the best jobs."

"One of the perks of being here the longest."

"Great." Clint hopped off the desk and looked down at Royce. "Seriously, Royce. Call him. The worst that's going to happen is he doesn't change his mind. Then you're still right where you are now, only you'll know if you could have done something."

"I don't want to get my hopes up," Royce admitted softly. It was hard to say, even to Clint, but it was the real reason he hadn't called. The situation right now sucked enough. He didn't want to make himself more vulnerable by putting himself out there like that.

"So don't. Apologize and see what happens. If nothing else, maybe you can save him as a customer." Clint pushed the phone back toward Royce. "Just call him."

"All right!" Royce picked up the phone, more because it would get Clint to leave than because he intended to call. "Get out so I can."

Clint tossed off a sloppy salute and left. As soon as the door clicked shut behind him, Royce put the phone down and turned back to the computer, determined to find something else to distract him.

Soon, it became apparent there was nothing else that needed Royce's attention at the moment, and he started wondering if prepping his taxes or rearranging the entire store would be more distracting. As soon as the thought registered, Royce gave it up as a losing battle, grabbed his phone, and headed upstairs. There was no possible way any conversation could be worse than moving thousands of wine bottles, but that didn't mean Royce wanted to have this conversation in the downstairs office, where anyone could have a reason to come in.

Upstairs, he slid his fingers across the screen of his phone before he had the chance to lose his courage and hit the green button next to Shawn's name on his contact list. As it rang, he vacillated between hoping Shawn would answer so he could figure this out and hoping the call would go to voice mail, so he could put the conversation off just a little bit longer. He was leaning toward voice mail when Shawn picked up. "Hello?"

"Hi." Royce walked over to his window and stared out at the gray sky as he tried to formulate his thoughts. Calling before he had a chance to think about it meant he hadn't chickened out, but it also meant he hadn't thought about how he wanted to phrase things.

"What do you want, Royce?"

Shawn sounded so weary and resigned that Royce had to bite back the urge to ask what was wrong. He knew what was wrong. He just hoped he wasn't about to add to the problem. "To apologize," he said, hoping that would keep Shawn on the phone long enough for them to actually talk. "You were right. Opening All Corked Up isn't the same thing as you buying your restaurant, and I don't know what you've done to get where you are. I shouldn't have assumed I did."

"Thanks. I appreciate it." Shawn paused. "Was there anything else?"

"I hoped we could talk about this." Royce missed the easy way their conversation had flown before. This felt wrong and awkward, and if he hadn't known they could talk for hours without things getting stilted, he never would have guessed it from how things felt now. "Did I interrupt something?"

"No, but there's nothing to talk about."

"Sure there is." Royce forced himself to stay positive He'd committed to doing what he could to make this right, and he wasn't going to give up that easily. "There's something here we can build on."

"I can't, remember?" Shawn sounded even more bitter than he had during their last conversation. The past three days clearly hadn't been good to him. "If I want to buy Delicto, I can't date you. I can't date anyone."

"Yes, you can. We just—"

"No." Shawn sighed. "Look, Royce, I appreciate you apologizing, I really do, but nothing has changed. I still want to buy Delicto and I'm not giving that up for anyone."

"I don't want you to." Royce turned so his back was to the window and sat on the wide sill. Usually, the cats loved it, but they were both elsewhere at the moment, a fact Royce was stupidly grateful for. He didn't need them distracting him right now. "We can be discreet. Your boss said he didn't want you flaunting stuff, right? So we order in, meet wherever we're going, or go to out of the way places. There are ways around it."

"So we'd just sneak around forever like a couple of teenagers trying to hide things from our parents?"

"Not forever. Just until you sign the paperwork."

"And what if we don't make it that long? What if we slip up and get caught? It's a great theory, but it's not practical, Royce. If something goes wrong, Henry could decide not to sell. I like you and maybe you're right. Maybe there is something to build on, but right now, there's nothing worth risking Delicto for."

He sounded genuinely regretful, but there was a firmness in his tone that let Royce know it wouldn't do him any good to push further. "All right, I won't push." he said, dropping the subject for the moment. "You'll call if you change your mind? I'm not going to sit around pining for you, but the shop keeps me busy. I might still be interested." The joke felt flat, but if he didn't rely on humor, Royce wasn't sure what he'd say.

"Of course."

The smile in Shawn's voice was obviously even more forced than Royce's, but Royce pretended he didn't notice.

"And stop by the shop if you want. Henry can't get mad at you for buying wine, and I know your sister wants to come to a tasting." They'd talked about that Friday night, so Royce wasn't sure Shawn would still be interested, but maybe if Shawn stopped by, they could start talking again.

"Henry can get mad about whatever he wants, but I'll mention the tasting to Megan. He'll have a hard time claiming it's a date if you're behind the bar and I'm with my sister."

One of the knots in Royce's stomach loosened at the idea that he'd at least get to see Shawn again. "Exactly." They'd talk at the tasting and maybe Shawn would change his mind. Maybe the affection would fade with time. It was impossible to tell, but at least this way they had a chance.

"I'll, uh, call the shop to register. After I talk to my sister."

"Yeah. Of course. I'll talk to you then. Or Clint or one of the girls will." Royce wasn't ready to stop even the stilted conversation they were having, but he knew better than to push it.

"Yeah," Shawn said softly, a more genuine smile in his voice now. "Thanks for calling, Royce"

"My pleasure. Take care."

"You too." Royce hung up the phone then, unable to stay on any longer without saying something he would regret. He put the phone down on the windowsill. The cats had wandered in during the conversation. "Well, I guess that went as well as could be expected," he said, as he sat down on the floor to pet them. Unfortunately, wasn't nearly as well as he had hoped.

8

"SHAWN!" Henry shuffled into the breakroom, where Shawn was reviewing the schedule for the evening, and scowled at him. "There's someone asking for you out front."

"There is?" Shawn wasn't expecting anyone. "Who?" He had a brief flash of hope it was Royce tracking him down despite his promise to leave Shawn alone, but he quickly suppressed it. The only communication he'd gotten from Royce in the past two weeks had been the All Corked Up newsletter. It was increasingly apparent Royce meant what he said, and if Shawn wanted to talk to him again, he'd have to make the first move.

"I don't know. Go see." Henry turned and shuffled out, heading toward the office. "Don't dawdle. Make them order something or leave."

"All right." Shawn had never been the type to have friends come hang out in Delicto while he worked, but ever since the conversation that had led to Shawn calling things off with Royce, Henry had treated him like he was a new employee who had no idea how to conduct himself at work. It galled him that Henry suddenly seemed to think he couldn't trust Shawn, but every time Henry said something that grated on Shawn's nerves, he reminded himself why he was doing this and that he wouldn't have to put up with it for too much longer.

Shawn headed to the front as soon as Henry was out of his way. He didn't run, but his curiosity about who could possibly be looking for him made his steps longer and faster than usual. There were very few people who stopped by to see him at work, and none of them should be here right now. His family was all at work, as were the guys he occasionally met for golf, and Anastasia was....

Anastasia was standing by the door with her hands tucked into jeans pockets, tapping one foot as she looked around. How she ever managed to stay still when the Navy required it, Shawn would never understand, because she was always moving when he saw her. Her face lit up with a wide grin when she saw him, and she bounced on her toes as though she wanted to launch herself across the room to tackle him.

Based on past experience, she probably did. Shawn was grateful she had enough sense not to fling herself at him while he was at work, but part of him wanted her to. He wouldn't admit it to anyone, not even the best friend he hadn't seen in seven months, but he needed a hug right now.

Since she clearly wasn't going to jump on him, Shawn threw decorum out the window, rushed over, and swung her around. "Anastasia! I thought you were on a boat somewhere!"

Anastasia laughed as Shawn set her down. "I was. We docked in Everett on Tuesday."

"You should have told me you were getting in. I would have come up."

"I can't, you know that. I'm not allowed to tell anyone where the boat is. The Navy didn't even tell our families until Sunday."

"Right. I forgot. You can't tell anyone because someone might not notice the giant aircraft carrier surrounded by smaller ships when they look out at the ocean." Shawn rolled his eyes. It was something they'd moaned about several times. "You should have had your mother tell me, then." He and Anastasia had been friends since their ill-advised attempt at a relationship in college before Shawn had admitted he was gay, and when he'd worried about coming out to his parents, hers had offered to take him in until he got on his feet if he needed it. Thankfully, it hadn't been necessary and he'd drifted away from Anastasia's family some, but they still usually kept him informed about where she was if she couldn't.

"I asked her not to. She didn't come up either. There was a Tiger Cruise from Hawai'i to San Diego, and some of them stayed on all the way to Everett, so it's been crazy. I had stuff to do before I could really visit. Besides, you've been quiet lately." She looked him up and down, somehow managing to make him feel smaller than she was despite only coming up to his shoulder. "I wanted to see how you were doing."

Shawn held his hands away from his sides and presented himself for inspection. "Do I pass?" He turned around slowly. "And what do you mean, *I've* been quiet? You've been on a boat! I couldn't talk to you!"

"You could e-mail. You used to e-mail. I've barely heard from you since Christmas, though."

"Sorry." She was right. He'd had other things on his mind this year. He'd considered e-mailing her about Royce and then about Henry, but she usually left the Internet-capable computers on the boat for sailors with kids at home, and sometimes it was weeks between his e-mail and her reply, so he hadn't bothered. "I didn't mean to worry you. I'm fine, though. Really."

"No, you're not. You're miserable, and we're going to talk about it as soon as you get off."

Shawn thought about protesting but stopped cold at the look on Anastasia's face. She was convinced and nothing he could say before Henry got too upset at him for chitchatting would change her mind. He'd probably only gotten away with talking to her for this long because Henry was shut in the office. If he came out and saw Shawn still standing around, he'd be in trouble.

"I'm stuck here for a few hours. It'll be seven thirty before I can get anywhere."

"That's fine. I'm going to stop in and see my mom." She stretched up and kissed him on the cheek. "Call me when you leave?"

"Yeah. Sure." Shawn squeezed Anastasia's shoulders. "I'll see you in a bit."

"Okay." Anastasia paused just before she reached the interior set of doors and gave him a look that dared him to disobey. "Don't forget to call."

"I won't," Shawn promised, his hand over his heart. "I swear. Now go. I'll talk to you later." He watched Anastasia leave then headed to the back, wondering how the conversation would go later. He was fine, really, but he doubted it would be easy to convince Anastasia of that.

ANASTASIA barely let Shawn get out of his car before she pounced on him on the sidewalk outside Vault Martini. He staggered back at the impact, amazed, as always, that she could pack so much force into such a tiny body, and wrapped his arms around her. "Damn, Stasia, I just saw you a couple hours ago."

"Not for long enough." She briefly tightened the hug, then stepped back and looked up at him with a critical expression. "And we definitely didn't talk like we need to."

Shawn had hoped she would forget about that. "I'm always happy to talk to you, Stasia, but I'm fine. Really. I don't know why you think I'm not."

"Because you've only called me Anastasia and Stasia since I got back." She looped her arm around his and pulled him toward the bar.

Damn. It hadn't even occurred to him to call her something else. He usually did it without thinking, and he silently cursed himself for it as she ordered them both martinis. It didn't mean anything was wrong, though, just that he was distracted. "So? That is your name, isn't it?"

"Yeah, but you only call me that around my parents. Usually you call me Anesthesia or Spacey Stacy or something like that."

"I can't have grown out of mean nicknames?"

"Nope." Anastasia picked a table in the back corner. "Not at the same time you stop e-mailing and start only posting game updates on Facebook."

"I've been busy!" He'd been working extra hard at Delicto ever since calling things off with Royce and trying very hard not to think about why. Facebook games had provided a good distraction in the evening and had the added bonus of letting his family know he was around and okay without him posting a real status update.

"Busy playing Bejeweled, maybe." Anastasia rolled her eyes. "Now, spill. What's wrong?"

"Nothing!" At least nothing he wanted to talk about the first night Anastasia was back in town.

"Fine. What's been going on the past few weeks?" She nudged his leg with her foot. "Come on. Something is going on with you. I want details."

"There's nothing going on! I—" Shawn withered under Anastasia's knowing glare. "I met a guy, all right? It's complicated."

"Okay. And?" Anastasia leaned forward eagerly. "I need details, Shawn."

"There really aren't any. We went on one date. He was great, but I can't see him anymore." He shrugged, trying to look nonchalant, but sure Anastasia would see through it. "I was a little caught up in it, that's all. It's over now, though, so I'll have plenty of time to e-mail and post on Facebook."

"Are you really that clueless or are you being deliberately obtuse just to annoy me?"

"Uh. What?" Shawn blinked at Anastasia in confusion as he tried to figure out what she meant. He could sort of see her point about him being distant lately, but he wouldn't be anymore. Anastasia would distract him from the whole situation with Royce and Henry much better than a Facebook game, and between the things he'd do with her and work, he wouldn't have a shortage of things to talk about either. "Genuinely clueless, I guess."

Anastasia's expression softened into something Shawn couldn't quite describe. "Oh, Shawn."

"What?"

"You know I'm not worried about whether or not you post on Facebook, right? I'm worried about why you're not posting there or e-mailing me or calling me crazy nicknames. Obviously, it has something to do with this guy you went on a date with. So why can't you see him again? And why don't you want to talk about it?"

"Because I can't change it, so what's the point in dwelling?" Shawn slumped in the booth, crossed his arms, and tried not to glare at Anastasia. "Henry said he wouldn't sell Delicto to me if I kept dating Royce, so I stopped. It's that simple."

"You just stopped dating him? Just like that?" Anastasia didn't look like she believed him. "You let Henry tell you how to run your personal life?"

"I'd gone on one date with the guy, Stasia. Talked to him, I don't know, five, maybe six times. We didn't have a profound bond or anything."

"Okay. Do you like him?"

"Yeah, but Henry said—"

"Henry is only your boss at work. He doesn't get to tell you what to do on your own time."

"No, but he does get to choose who to sell to. I've been saving for this for years, Stasia, you know that. I can't let him decide not to sell to me because I clicked with some cute guy."

Anastasia frowned. "Fine. So you're just going to let Henry run your life for, what, the next year?"

"Something like that," Shawn muttered, though that really wasn't his plan. Henry wasn't going to run his life. He just was going to respect Henry's wishes about dating.

"And what happens if something goes wrong and you can't afford to buy it in a year? What then? How long do you let him run your life? How long do you put off other things you want?"

Shawn's stomach clenched at the thought. "That won't happen."

"What if it does? Is owning Delicto someday really worth putting off everything else you want?" She slid out of the booth and looked down at Shawn. "Think about it. I'm going to get another drink."

Shawn drained the dregs off his martini and slammed the glass back on the table. Sometimes he hated talking to Anastasia about his problems. She had a way of cutting through to the heart of the issue and ignoring all the extraneous stuff that distracted him. It was helpful but sometimes made him feel like an idiot and left him wondering how he'd missed the obvious. He had thought this was a cut-and-dried issue: his years-long desire to own Delicto versus his attraction to a guy he barely knew. Looking at it that way, there was no choice. Delicto won, hands down, and there was no reason for Shawn to think about Royce anymore. Anastasia's view of one particular desire versus overall happiness put it in a different light. Shawn wasn't sure he completely agreed with Anastasia, but it did explain why he hadn't been able to stop thinking about Royce.

He spun his glass between his fingers and mulled over what Anastasia had said as he watched the glass wobble. Three weeks ago, he would have scoffed at the idea that Henry would even consider not selling Delicto to him, for any reason, but now he wondered if Henry wasn't actively looking for one. Shawn didn't want to think it was a possibility, but he could imagine Henry refusing to sell even after he had all the money. He would have a reason, of course, one Shawn couldn't argue against, but he'd keep coming up with them until Shawn gave up or someone came along with an offer Shawn couldn't match.

"Damn," Shawn muttered. "She's right."

"What was that?" Another martini appeared in from of Shawn, and he silently cursed Anastasia's impeccable timing

"I said you were right," he repeated a little louder. "It's not as cut-and-dried as I thought."

"Obviously." Anastasia slid into the booth and peered at Shawn over the top of her martini glass. "What are you going to do about it?"

"I don't know." Shawn took a long drink of his martini and silently cursed Anastasia's choice in beverages. He would much rather have been drinking beer for this conversation. "I like Royce, but I'm not ready to give up on the idea of owning Delicto, even if Henry is looking for a reason not to sell to me. I don't think I will be until he flat-out tells me I can't buy it."

"I didn't say you should give up on it. Just that you should think about other things too. Like this Royce guy, for instance." Anastasia leaned in and grinned conspiratorially. "Come on, tell me about him. What's he like? How'd you meet? I need the scoop!"

Shawn thought about protesting for approximately half a second before he realized there was no possible way he would get away with anything less than the full story. He could probably distract Anastasia for a while by asking about her time on the cruise, but he suspected she'd tell him it was a lot like the last few times and change the subject right back to Royce. If he wanted to know more than vague secondhand details about what she'd been doing for the last seven months—and he did—he would have to give her what she wanted first. "He owns a wine shop, actually. All Corked

Up. I met him on Christmas Eve when I was looking for wine to take to dinner at Karen's."

As he talked, Shawn started to settle and he automatically fell into his regular rhythm of conversation with Anastasia. By the time he got to the part of the story where they kissed in front of the wine shop, he was grinning and waving his hands as he spoke. "And after, when he was going inside, he—"

Anastasia grabbed his martini glass just before he knocked it over. "So what I'm getting is you like this guy."

Shawn took his glass back from Anastasia. "Yeah." It was scary how much, especially after a rocky start and two weeks with no communication. "I do."

"So do something about it. Call him. Ask him out again. Tell him you want to try to sneak around like teenagers behind your parents' backs."

"He suggested that already. I turned him down."

"Why would you do that?" Anastasia held up a hand before Shawn could say anything. "No, don't answer that."

"Okay." Shawn didn't want to. He doubted the real answer was flattering.

"You should tell him you changed your mind. Call him up, say you thought about it, and you want to give it a shot. If you're lucky, he'll still be interested."

"I'll think about it." This time, it was Shawn's turn to stop Anastasia from saying anything. "Seriously. I'll think about it, but I'm not going to make a decision right now."

"Fair enough. I'll leave it be for now." Anastasia gave Shawn a calculating look. "I'm not going to let it drop forever, though."

Shawn had no doubt about that. "I'm aware of that. Now, tell me about the cruise. Did you see anything new?"

"Not that I hadn't told you about already," Anastasia groused, but she smiled as she said it, and she didn't need any encouragement to start a story Shawn hadn't yet heard.

9

SHAWN paused just inside the door of All Corked Up and looked around the room as he tried to gather his courage. The same two women he remembered working the bar in the front room last time were there again, serving the small crowd of people gathered around them. There was a line at the front counter too, obscuring Shawn's view of who was behind it. He assumed it was Clint, but he hasn't arrived from the right side to look through the window, so it could be Lisa, another employee Shawn hadn't met, or—heaven help them both—Royce.

"Move." Anastasia squeezed through the door behind him and maneuvered him into the room with her hands on his hips. "It's not polite to stop just inside a door."

"Sorry," Shawn said reflexively as he stepped further into the room. From this angle, he could see Clint behind the counter and though he was glad it wasn't Royce, Shawn wasn't sure he was ready to deal with Clint, either.

Anastasia stood next to him and stretched up on her toes to stare over the heads of the people in front of the counter. "What are we looking at?"

"Just seeing who's there." Shawn fought the urge to leave. He'd promised Anastasia she could come when Megan backed out after he bought the tickets, and he'd never hear the end of it if he made her leave now. He was an adult. They were all adults. He could do this.

"Is that him?" Anastasia cocked her head and looked at Clint critically. "Can't be. You said he was tall and pretty. That guy is short, and he's hot, but I wouldn't call him pretty."

"That's Clint, his best friend. He's probably more likely to give me grief than Royce is, to be honest. But we're not getting back to Royce without checking in first, and that means going through Clint."

"Ohhh. A gauntlet." Anastasia sounded far too thrilled by that idea. "Come on. Let's see if we can pass the test and get into the secret lair."

"It's not a—" Shawn shook his head as he let Anastasia lead him to the counter. "You spend far too much time reading fantasy books."

"No such thing." Anastasia kept a firm grip on Shawn's arm as they reached the front of the line. When Clint looked up, she bounced on her toes and smiled warmly. "Hi! We need to check in."

"Sure. What's the—Oh. Hello, Shawn." Clint's tone cooled to just the right side of polite when he noticed Shawn. "Royce wasn't sure you were going to come."

"I bought tickets."

"We sometimes get people who don't show up." Clint's smile looked forced, and he quickly shifted his gaze back to Anastasia. "Is this your sister?"

"No. My sister couldn't come. This is my friend—"

"Anastasia Carnes. The person who tries to wrangle sense into this guy here." She bumped her shoulder against Shawn as she held out her hand to Clint. "Sorry he's been an idiot. I was on an aircraft carrier."

"Ah! That explains it." Clint shook Anastasia's hand heartily. "Clint Derwalt. I do the same for Royce, though he's kept me busy running the shop lately."

"Oh yeah. That *is* a problem."

"Tell me about it. I tried to wrangle them both, but...."

Anastasia winced. "Yeah. I get it. Shawn is bad enough on his own."

"Hey!"

"I say that with love, Shawn." Anastasia spared him a glance them turned back to Clint. "Sometimes he's great, but sometimes he gets an idea in his head—"

"And you just can't get it out."

"Are you two going to do this all night?" Shawn was starting to feel like he was at a tennis match watching the two of them volley. "I thought we came to drink wine."

"I thought you came to flirt with Royce," Anastasia countered.

"He's in the other room." Clint handed Shawn a glass. "Go show him he was wrong about you skipping out."

Shawn took the glass and let Anastasia shoo him into the other room. He was torn about her staying behind to talk to Clint. On the one hand, it gave him a chance to try to apologize to Royce without her hovering. On the other, she and Clint were getting along like a house on fire and he really didn't want to think about what that might mean for him and Royce. Both Clint and Anastasia were forces to be reckoned with alone. Shawn shuddered to think what they could do together.

He saw Royce as soon as he stepped through the door to the other room, standing in the same spot he'd occupied last time, pouring wine for the line of customers. There weren't as many people as last time, but there were enough to keep Royce occupied, and he seemed oblivious to Shawn's presence as he hovered at the end of the snack table.

For a moment, he thought about leaving before Royce noticed him, but even as he considered it, he knew he couldn't. Even if Anastasia let him get away with it, which was unlikely, Clint knew he was here. He would mention it to Royce, who would wonder why Shawn had left, and Shawn wouldn't get another chance. Besides, he'd come here with a plan and he'd be damned if he wasn't going to stick to it.

He took the long way to the bar so he could stop at the food table on the way and eliminate his last possible excuse to leave once he got there. Once he'd filled a plate, he eyed the line, figured out it was mostly people milling around and not people actually waiting for wine, and headed to the end of the bar closest to Royce. The butterflies in his stomach looped, but he ignored them and took up the same position he'd occupied the last time he was here. "Hi."

Royce looked genuinely shocked for a brief moment before his expression settled into one of polite surprise. "You came," he said in a tone even cooler than Clint's had been. "I didn't think you would."

"I bought tickets," Shawn pointed out in a slightly exasperated tone. "I don't know why you'd think I would buy tickets and not come."

"People do. Things come up, and we just keep the money on their accounts until they use it." Royce shrugged. "I figured you'd decide Henry might not approve of you coming here either and it wasn't worth the risk."

Shawn deserved that and he knew it, but Royce's biting tone still hurt. "No. I'm not going to let him dictate my life that much."

"He just gets to dictate your romantic life, then."

"No. Well." Shawn sighed. This conversation wasn't going at all how he'd imagined it. "I wanted to talk to you about that, actually. When you have a minute."

He gestured to the customers approaching the bar with empty glasses and stood back so he wouldn't be in the way. The few customers turned into a wave as groups of people finished their wine, and for about five minutes Shawn stood back, watching and wondering if he shouldn't have skipped tonight after all.

Royce interacted with his customers easily, showing none of the coolness that had characterized his conversation with Shawn so far. Instead, he smiled and laughed, his eyes sparkling and his voice warm as he talked about the wine he poured. It was fascinating to watch, but it left Shawn aching to have some of that warmth directed his way instead of the coolness he knew would return as soon as Royce turned his attention back to him.

When the line dwindled enough that Shawn didn't feel bad distracting Royce, he stepped up to the bar again and put his plate back down on the edge of it. "I'm sorry," he said the moment Royce's attention was back on him.

Royce's expression softened slightly, but his tone stayed cool. "For what?"

"Being an idiot?" Shawn laughed, though there was little humor in it. "For panicking, I guess. For blowing you off so easily." He looked down at his empty wine glass. This would be easier with some liquid courage, but he didn't want to stop now to ask for some. He might never start again. "I've put all my energy for the past several years into the idea of owning Delicto someday, and I can't give up on that. But I can't—I shouldn't—let Henry dictate what I can and can't do outside of work, either. And I did, and that means I blew you off even when you wanted to work around Henry, and I'm sorry."

"Thanks." Royce's tone was warmer now, though nothing like the friendly exuberance he was using with the other customers.

It was enough, though, to give Shawn a glimmer of hope, and he sucked in a deep breath and pushed forward before he lost his nerve. "I was wondering if you would still be willing to give it a try. The being discreet thing." He ignored Royce's dubious expression and plowed through, determined not to stop until he was done. "I thought a lot about what you said, and Anastasia smacked me upside the head until I admitted it, but you were right. There was—is?—something here we could build on. I'd like to try."

Royce went straight for his wine and swallowed what was left of his glass before he refilled it from the decanter at the end of the bar. He held it out to Shawn questioningly, and Shawn nodded, not about to turn down alcohol to help this conversation along. "Thanks."

"Sure." Royce managed a smile that didn't look entirely forced. "You paid for it, after all. I should have started you on the first one, actually."

"It's fine," Shawn said automatically and took a sip of his wine to stop himself from saying something he'd regret. It was surprisingly good, and he indulged in a few more sips before setting it down. He didn't want to push the issue, but he wouldn't be able to enjoy the tasting until he got an answer. It would be better to get it done before Anastasia finished bonding with Clint and came to force the issue. "So, uh. What do you think?"

Royce set his wine glass down with a sigh. "I don't know, Shawn. I—" He broke off as an older gentleman approached the counter. "Hello, what can I get for you?"

Shawn looked toward the other room as he waited for Royce to finish with the customer. It was hard to tell from this angle, but it looked like Anastasia was still leaning against the front counter talking to Clint about Lord knew what at this point. Whatever it was, it couldn't be good for him or for Royce, and Shawn dreaded what would happen if they finished their conversation before he and Royce finished theirs. He wanted to ask Royce to step away from the bar for a minute so they could talk without being interrupted, but he doubted he'd get the answer he wanted, and he didn't want to jinx the rest of the conversation by starting down that path.

By the time the man stepped away, a woman was waiting behind him, and Shawn ended up waiting through three more customers before he could command Royce's attention again. "You what?" he asked softly, hoping Royce hadn't lost his train of thought.

"I can't do this if you're going to run again at the first sign Henry might know something."

Shawn's stomach clenched at the idea. "I thought you were willing to—"

"Be discreet, yeah. I am. But discreet doesn't mean invisible." Royce glanced out over the room then turned and looked Shawn straight in the eyes. "We can go down to Eugene or out to the vineyards for every date, if you want, but there's still a chance someone could see us. Hell, we could stay in all the time and someone might comment on how often you come here or see my car parked on your street and put two and two together. I have to know you're okay with that, or there's no point in trying."

Shawn willed the butterflies in his stomach to stop fluttering around and met Royce's gaze evenly. "And if I am?"

"I'd say one of the vineyards I buy from has a tour I've been meaning to go on and point out the chances of someone seeing us on a Portland Underground tour are slim." He smiled, just a small one, but warmer than any look he'd granted Shawn all night. "I'd mention I'm not very familiar with restaurants in Eugene but I'm sure we could find a nice one."

Shawn matched Royce's smile as he relaxed for the first time that night. "And if I were to respond that I am an excellent cook and I've always wanted to go on the Portland Underground tour?"

"I'd ask how next Saturday sounded."

Shawn had hoped for tomorrow so he wouldn't have a chance to second-guess his decision, but it was probably better to wait a week. It would echo their first date less, for one, and it would give Shawn time to clean and time to spend with Anastasia while she was in town. "I'd say it sounds great."

This time, Royce graced Shawn with his real smile, the one he'd been flashing at customers all night as he explained their wine to them. "It's a date." He looked around again and seemed to realize for the first time that Shawn was alone. "Where's your sister? I thought she was coming with you."

"Her friend got tickets to a concert at Dante's tonight. She went there instead. It offered more opportunities for her to get drunk and throw herself at pseudocelebrities." Shawn was too relieved Royce was making an effort to have normal conversation to worry about Megan's dignity. It was her fault for abandoning him, anyway. She deserved whatever he dished out. "I brought my friend Anastasia instead."

Royce regarded him dubiously. "And where is she?"

"Out front." Now that he wasn't trying to keep the conversation flowing around customers, Shawn stepped away from the bar long enough to look into the other room. Sure enough, Anastasia was still leaning on the front counter, laughing as Clint talked and waved his hands. "She's plotting with Clint."

"Plotting?"

"Yeah." Shawn shook his head as he returned to his position at the side of the bar. "Anastasia is very... focused. She thinks she knows what's best for me, and she never hesitates to tell me when I'm wrong."

Royce chuckled. "Sounds like Clint. The two of them together could be dangerous."

"You have no idea." Shawn was still trying very hard not to think about what Anastasia and Clint were plotting. "Stasia can come on strong, too, especially when she hasn't been around for a while. She's in the Navy. Even stationed in Everett, it's hard to get away sometimes, and she just got back from a seven-month cruise."

"Should I worry?"

"About her teaming up with Clint? Maybe." Shawn resisted the urge to look again. He wouldn't be able to tell what they were talking about without getting a lot closer, and they'd stop talking about it before he could. "They're probably trying to figure out how to get us to go on another date."

"Really." Royce's grin was positively evil. He scanned the crowd, told Lisa he'd be back, and stepped out from behind the bar. "Why don't you introduce me? I want to see if they try anything."

Shawn grinned. "All right." He didn't get to pull things over on Anastasia very often. This was going to be fun.

10

THE MAX got him to Hobo's just in time, five minutes before the arranged meeting time for their tour, fifteen minutes before the actual tour was scheduled to start. Royce had suggested they meet earlier and grab a bite before the tour started, but Shawn had thought about someone walking into the restaurant and seeing him dining with Royce again and refused. There was also a bar closely tied to the Portland Underground tours. Maybe, if things went well on the tour of the tunnels, he'd consider grabbing a drink with Royce there afterward. The later it was, the less likely they were to run into someone Henry knew well, and a bar was a much less likely venue for any of Henry's friends than a restaurant.

Royce was leaning against a wall near the Portland Underground meeting area when Shawn arrived. He had his hands shoved into the pockets of dark jeans that hugged his legs in a way than made Shawn want to take the time to properly appreciate them, and his dark green shirt brought out flecks of color in his eyes Shawn had never noticed before. His Doc Martens were practical for walking in old underground tunnels, as was the thick material of his shirt and the light black jacket he wore open over it, but the practicality of his ensemble did nothing to detract from his attractiveness. Even dressed for an underground hike, Royce looked more put-together than most of the people in the restaurant, and Shawn would happily have stared at him all day.

He let himself stare for the time it took him to cross the restaurant, then cleared his throat when he was within speaking distance. "Hi."

"Hey! You made it!" Royce looked pleased—though a little surprised—to see him.

Shawn tried not to let that hurt. He'd asked for it by backing off because of Henry. He needed to earn Royce's trust again, and it wouldn't be as easy this time around. "Yeah. I didn't want to be too early. Waiting around with nothing to do isn't my idea of a good time."

"Mine either, usually, but the downtime was nice today. I feel like I've been running around for a week."

"Is the store that busy?" Shawn knew Royce was doing well, but he couldn't imagine All Corked Up having so many customers Royce didn't get any downtime. Even on the busiest days at Delicto, Shawn could always find a few minutes to rest, and Royce could pass off more of his responsibilities than Shawn could.

"No." Royce shook his head. "It's steady, but we're never swamped unless there's a tasting. I've been meeting with lawyers and loan officers. That sort of fun thing."

"Why?" Sudden worry coiled in Shawn's gut. He *thought* Royce was doing well, anyway. "The store isn't in trouble, is it?"

He winced as soon as he said it, but Royce laughed. "God, no. I'm looking at expanding, actually. I want to add a restaurant in the unused building space, but there are a lot of logistics to figure out."

Shawn was tempted to offer his expertise if Royce needed help getting the actual restaurant set up, but he hesitated, afraid Henry would find even that a violation of their agreement. He was still looking closely at everything Shawn did, and while Shawn felt brave enough to covertly date, he knew there was no way Henry would miss the amount of time he'd have to spend at All Corked Up in order to properly help.

Before Shawn could decide if it was worth the risk to offer, the tour guide called the group together and Shawn stopped thinking about it so he could at least sort of pay attention to the speech she gave. He was only mildly interested in the presentation beyond the basic safety instructions, but Royce was fascinated and hung on the guide's every word.

When she stopped to hand out the flashlights that would light the infamous Shanghai Tunnels for them, Shawn bumped Royce's shoulder. "You really like this stuff, huh?"

"It's fascinating. And a little scary." Royce grinned. "Can you imagine going out for a drink and ending up trapped under the city instead? It took those men years to get home once they were sold onto ships!"

"I try not to think about it, actually." The Shanghai Tunnels, while interesting, were not the high point of Portland's history. Able-bodied men had had been tricked into falling though trapdoors in the waterfront, held in underground cells until they were needed, then drugged and transferred onto ships. By the time they woke up, the ships were out at sea and they had no choice but to work as part of the crew. "It's kind of terrifying to think that the tunnels are still there."

Royce laughed. "You do realize you're about to go into them, right?"

"It's not going into them that bothers me. It's the idea of walking into a bar, falling through a trapdoor, and spending the next several years in forced labor. You can't tell me that idea doesn't bother you."

"It would if it still happened. Really, I just think it's fascinating it went on for so long." Royce shrugged. "It's like a car crash. It's terrible, but it happened to someone else, so you want to look and see what you can. Besides, the tunnels weren't just used to kidnap crews for ships. Bars relocated underground during Prohibition."

Shawn shook his head. "You really *are* into this, aren't you?"

"I'm a history buff. It kind of goes with the wine thing. If you learn about the history of a varietal, you learn about the history of the region it's grown in too." Royce flashed a half smile and shrugged one shoulder. "I get more into it than most people. Sorry."

"Don't be. I think it's fun. I just wouldn't have picked history as one of your hobbies, that's all."

The group moved forward, heading into the tunnels. Neither Royce nor Shawn had been given a flashlight as they were only handed out to every fourth person, but Shawn didn't mind. It would have been nice to direct the beam where they wanted it to go so they could see everything, but this way they didn't have people clustering around them, wanting to share the light. They could hang back a little if they wanted and take advantage of the shadows.

"I didn't used to be," Royce said as he ducked through the entrance. "I liked it well enough, but I was more like you, just casually interested and not really into it." He paused and looked worriedly at Shawn. "You *are* at least casually interested, right?"

"I wouldn't have said I wanted to come if I wasn't." Shawn had been willing to compromise on a lot to get Royce to give him another chance, but he still wouldn't have agreed to do something he had no interest in at all. He had enough experience to know that wouldn't end well, and he wanted this to work.

"Good." Royce sounded pleased. "Anyway, when I opened All Corked Up, I didn't really have any free time. I couldn't keep up with current authors or the latest trends, but every time I picked up a history book, I could start right where I left off and I wasn't any further behind than I'd been when I put it down."

"Things still happen," Shawn pointed out quietly. "People make history all the time."

"Yes, but I wasn't reading about current events. I was reading about stuff that happened in the past. I could pick my books, and even if a new one got published, there wasn't much chance it would have new information in it."

"So if you've read everything on the Shanghai Tunnels, why are we here?"

"Because it's a different perspective. Different presentations mean you pick up different information." Royce nudged Shawn as the guide told the group to stop. "Now, listen. You might find something interesting."

Shawn grinned and turned toward the guide. He was sure he'd find something about the tour interesting. He just wasn't sure it would be anything the guide told him.

SHAWN squeezed Royce's hand as they exited the tunnels, then let go and stepped away slightly. He'd gotten brave about halfway through the tour and taken it in the dark, but here in the lighted room where there was a chance they might be seen, he wasn't ready yet. He was feeling braver than he had when he'd arrived, though, so he slipped his hands into his pockets and rocked back on his heels when the tour had officially ended. "Do you want to check out the bar they mentioned?"

Royce tucked his hands into his jacket pockets. "We can," he said slowly, "though we might have better luck if we head out of Old Town. The bars around here tend to be pretty sketchy."

"True." That had been part of the appeal—the chances he'd run into someone who knew Henry were slimmer in Old Town—but he wanted to be able to talk to Royce too. "Where do you think we should go?"

"Rontoms, maybe?" Royce shrugged as they stepped out of Hobo's and onto the street. "We could stop and get food too, if we're hungry later."

"Or drunk?"

"Maybe," Royce conceded as he headed away from the restaurant toward Rontoms, "but I don't plan to get drunk. I have to open the store in the morning."

"And I have to open Delicto." The thought of the restaurant killed some of Shawn's good mood. He still liked the place, but a lot of the joy of working there had faded over the past few weeks. On multiple occasions, he'd had to remind himself that when he bought it, Henry wouldn't be able to question his every move anymore and he wouldn't have to fight to do things extra well just to get Henry to think he was doing okay.

"You don't sound too thrilled about that."

Of course Royce would notice. "Henry's been coming in earlier lately." He left the *since our first date* unsaid, but he could tell Royce knew.

"He doesn't trust you." Disapproval was clear in Royce's voice. "But you still want to buy from him?"

"When I buy it from him, he won't be there." Shawn stopped on the corner and took a deep breath. The idea of heading up Couch to the MAX station at 5th and Couch occurred to him, but he pushed it out of his mind as he tried to let go of his irritation. He'd decided he wanted to see where this could go, and he couldn't do that by running away just because Royce didn't understand one thing. "Do you want to walk or take the bus?"

"Let's walk. It's not that far."

Rontoms was about a fifteen-minute walk across the river, but unless they caught the bus at exactly the right time, they wouldn't save any time by taking it. "Okay."

It was a nice night, cool enough Shawn was glad he was wearing his jacket, but warmer than usual for a mid-March evening. As they strolled down Burnside, he kept his hands in his pockets and reminded himself several times that he couldn't reach out to take Royce's hand. Not here where anyone could see them.

His fingers twitched seemingly of their own volition as they crossed the Willamette. The river was picturesque, with a good view of Portland at night on both sides. The romantic thing to do would be to hold hands as they crossed, maybe even stop to kiss like the couple crossing in the other direction. As he made a fist in his pocket and stepped slightly further away from Royce to avoid temptation, Shawn vowed to find a dark corner where he could feel safe enough to take Royce's hand at Rontoms.

Royce closed the gap Shawn had put between them until they were again walking close enough their shoulders were almost touching. "You know, most people don't analyze how far apart other people are."

"Most people aren't trying to figure out if someone is breaking the rules their boss laid down." Shawn kicked a loose rock over the edge of the bridge. It fell into the river below with a soft splash. "If any of Henry's friends see us, they will be."

"If any of Henry's friends see us, they're already going to report to Henry that you're out with another guy." Royce stepped away so there was slightly more than a foot between them again. "Isn't that what Henry's really worried about?"

He had a point, and it almost made Shawn regret agreeing to continue their date outside the Shanghai Tunnels. "Yeah, but if we're not pressed closer together, I can try to claim we're just friends." He wasn't sure Henry would believe him or even care about the distinction at this point, but it gave Shawn something to cling to as he tried to figure out if Royce was worth risking Henry's wrath.

"Try to claim? That doesn't sound like you think you'll be successful."

"Like I said, Henry's been watching me extra closely. You're right. I don't think he trusts me anymore." They stopped on a corner to wait for the light to change. "I'm not sure I can convince him. He's all about what people think, and he's convinced I'll destroy the reputation of the restaurant if I'm seen on a date with another guy."

"Because no guy ever just goes out to the bar with his guy friends," Royce said sarcastically as they walked through the door at Rontoms. "Clearly, every person here is on a date."

"I know, all right? Henry just doesn't—He's a product of his time, that's all." Shawn sighed. This wasn't how he wanted the evening to go. "Sorry. I know it's ridiculous and I'm probably being paranoid, but I have to work for the guy. It's already hard enough. Can we just find a table?"

"Sure." Thankfully, Royce didn't push the issue. "You want to grab one while I get drinks?"

Shawn saw a table in the back that looked out of the way enough that he thought he might be comfortable risking a little physical contact with Royce if the evening went that way. Ten minutes ago, he'd been sure that it would and he would have thought the table was about perfect. Now, all it offered was a chance, but Shawn had to take it. Henry had already influenced their date enough. "Yeah. Grab me whatever you're getting. I'm gonna head over there."

"Sure. I'll be over in a minute."

Shawn watched Royce walk away, admiring the way his jeans clung to his ass, then claimed the table. It was in just about the perfect spot. As he sat down, Shawn decided he would take advantage of that, assuming Royce still wanted him to. He would never figure out anything if he didn't take a chance.

11

"SO HOW'D it go last night?"

Royce should have known better than to expect Clint would wait to ask about his date, but it still threw him off to be questioned before his coffee kicked in. He'd forgotten Clint would be here this morning. Royce usually opened alone on days he took the early shift, but Clint had offered to come in a couple of hours early today in case Royce was out late enough he couldn't get up at a reasonable hour. "Good morning to you too."

Clint was unfazed. "Someone's grumpy. Does that mean last night was awful or awesome?"

Royce glared, but it was obvious Clint wasn't going to give up without an answer. "Neither." He rubbed his eyes to try to wake up a little. "It was good. Not awesome. But not awful, either. We had a nice time."

"Just nice?" Clint sounded disappointed. "I thought you said there was something between you two. Hell, I thought there was something between you two. What happened?"

"Nothing happened." Royce went behind the counter and started opening the register. It was futile to hope Clint would leave him alone because he was busy, but it would give him a reason to take a little time answering. Maybe he could slow the barrage of questions he knew were coming. "We had a perfectly nice evening. Shawn's just worried about Henry, so we're being cautious, that's all."

Clint joined him behind the counter and started opening the other register. "Too cautious?"

Royce had thought that at a few points last night, but he'd agreed to it when he decided to give Shawn another chance. "Maybe a little. But only sometimes." Shawn had held his hand during the tour of the tunnels and again at Rontoms, though only in short bursts in the bar. "He's trying."

"For now." They'd never get anywhere if Shawn stayed this skittish about being affectionate or even being seen with Royce, but this was the first time they'd gone out since Henry threatened Shawn. Royce didn't expect a miracle and didn't know if he wanted one. Shawn wasn't the only one figuring out where he wanted this to go.

Clint looked shrewdly at Royce for a moment, then nodded, apparently satisfied with what he saw. "So when's the next date?"

Royce laughed. Of course Clint assumed they'd have another date. Sometimes Royce thought Clint was more invested in his relationship than he was. "We talked about next weekend, not that it's any of your business."

Clint took it as the joke it was and chuckled. "Of course it's my business. I can't live vicariously through you if I don't have details. It's your obligation as my friend to provide them."

"Uh-huh." He was going to tell Clint, of course—he didn't really have anyone else to tell unless he wanted to discuss his dating life with his family—but he wasn't going to give in so easily. "It's my obligation as your boss to tell you I need you to close on Saturday. I don't have to tell you why."

"So, Saturday, huh?" Clint finished with the register and went over to the bar toward the back of the room. "Where you going to take him?"

Royce followed, more so he wouldn't have to yell across the shop than because there was anything he needed to do. Clint had already taken care of most of the opening work. "I thought we'd go out to Heartwood Vineyards."

"On a *date*?" Clint looked aghast. "You go out there for work. You can't take Shawn there on a date."

"I'm not taking him to see what new wines they have to offer me." Although, if Shawn enjoyed learning about wine as much as he claimed he did, he'd probably enjoy that. Maybe someday Royce would invite him along. Saturday, however, was going to be a date, not a work trip. "They have tours and a restaurant. I thought I'd get someone to show us around the vineyard and have dinner without worrying about who we're going to run into."

"Avoiding Henry, huh?" Clint looked at Royce knowingly. "Hoping for a little more action on the next date?"

It sounded crude when Clint put it like that, but it was accurate. Out of the city, Shawn would have no reason to think they'd run into Henry or anyone he knew. They'd be able to relax and just be on a date rather than constantly think about other, less pleasant things. "Well, I'm not going to put it like that."

"Obviously. But that is what you want, right?"

"I want to get to know him better." If that involved a little more touching and kissing and maybe more, Royce wouldn't object, but mostly he wanted to see what they had the potential to be. If they had to take it slow, well, he'd been satisfying himself with his hands and toys for longer than he cared to think about. He'd last a few more weeks.

"That's one way to put it, I suppose." Clint leaned against the bar. "You are going to share what happens when you don't have to worry about what might get back to his boss, right? I was serious about the living vicariously thing."

"You could always try dating someone, you know." Royce kept his tone dry. He knew Clint wouldn't appreciate sympathy, but he also knew Clint was at least partially serious about living vicariously. His last relationship had ended badly before he'd moved to Portland and started working at All Corked Up. Royce had seen Clint flirt plenty and knew he hooked up with people sometimes, but he'd never seen Clint in a relationship.

"In my plethora of spare time?" Clint's sarcasm was almost overwhelming. It made Royce regret making the suggestion. "No, thanks. I'm too busy."

"Doing what? I thought you hadn't found another house to flip yet." If Clint hadn't been such a good friend, Royce would have despaired at his constantly changing address. He flipped houses—lived in them as he renovated, and then sold them for a nice profit. He only worked at All Corked Up to have steady income for day-to-day expenses. Royce could see how between flipping a house and putting in hours at the shop, Clint wouldn't have time for much of a social life, but if he wasn't currently renovating, he should have plenty of free time.

"I haven't been looking for another house to flip. I told you I'd use the money from selling this house to add the restaurant on if you hadn't found another investor yet. I can't do that if I use it to buy another house."

"So then why are you too busy?"

"I'll be spending more time here." Clint rolled his eyes. He hadn't said "idiot," but Royce heard it anyway. "I'm not going to invest and then be hands-off."

That was one plus of the offer Royce wasn't sure he wanted to accept. On the one hand, Royce trusted Clint and knew they worked well together. He knew Clint would care about how the project turned out, that he was good for the money, and that he would have a realistic expectation for how quickly his investment would be repaid. On the other hand, All Corked Up wasn't Clint's passion—flipping houses was—and he had no experience with the restaurant business. Royce was also sure Clint would pull out of the day-to-day stuff after a few years and go back to flipping houses, which would leave Royce okay financially, but he'd struggle with managing things.

"All right, I'll drop it." Royce held up his hands in surrender to lighten the mood. "You don't get to experience everything vicariously, though. I'm not telling you everything."

"You'll tell me most of it," Clint said, relaxing a little. "I expect juicy details next Sunday, and a lot more when I get back."

"Get back?" Royce didn't remember Clint telling him anything about leaving. He'd been planning to ask Clint to pick up some hours over the next few weeks so he could have more delightful discussions with bankers and lawyers. "What do you mean, get back?"

"Uh. Yeah." Clint rubbed the back of his neck. "I was gonna mention that today. My mom called last night. She's having surgery on the fourth and she wants me to come stay with her for a couple of weeks. She'll have painkillers and she won't be allowed to drive so she needs someone to chauffeur her around and make sure she doesn't do anything stupid while she's doped up. I got nominated."

Royce could hardly tell Clint he couldn't go stay with his mother when she was having surgery, so he made a mental note to revise his plans for the next few weeks. "Is she all right? Is it something serious?"

"Gall bladder." Clint shrugged. "She told me she'll be fine, it's not a big deal, yadda, yadda, but she wants me to come. I can't really say no."

Royce wouldn't either. "Right. Well, let me know when you're leaving and coming back as soon as you know, so I can schedule around it. And, uh, pass my best wishes on to your mother."

"Of course." Clint looked like he was searching for a way to change the subject—something Royce would have welcomed as well—when the door leading upstairs creaked open and Kirra tumbled out. Clint laughed as she scrambled to her feet and tried to look like she'd intended to roll down the stairs. "You're going to have to train her to stay out of the shop."

"Why?" Royce obediently picked Kirra up when she chirped at him. "The customers love her. She has no desire to go outside. And she knows not to get on the bars. It's no different than Puck coming down."

"Except for the part where Puck isn't a rambunctious kitten who zooms all over the place and hides in the wine." Clint reached over the bar to scratch Kirra behind her ears. "She's a menace." The tone of his voice softened as he looked down at Kirra. "A cute menace, but still a menace."

"She's not a menace, she's a sweetheart. Aren't you, girl?" Royce rubbed Kirra's belly, and she squirmed and chirped at him. "Besides, Puck hides in the wine too. I found him sleeping in the Spanish section yesterday."

Clint pulled his hand back as Kirra batted at it. "Puck doesn't zoom around like Speedy Gonzales on crack, though. Half the time, I'm afraid she's going to break something!"

Royce shrugged. Wine bottles were sturdier than they looked and most of them weighed more than Kirra did. He was more worried about one falling on her than her breaking one. "Puck is older. Kirra will calm down eventually. Besides, my kitten, my store. I think I'll manage if she knocks something over." Kirra started squirming and Royce put her down so she could explore. "I'll have to keep them upstairs once we open the restaurant unless we keep it completely separate from the store so they can't get in, but there's no harm in letting them come down now."

"I suppose. You're going to break their hearts if you start locking them upstairs once we open the restaurant, though."

"They'll live," Royce said dryly. He had no doubt they'd drive him nuts trying to get downstairs for a while, but they'd get used to it eventually.

"Or we'll figure out how to keep the cats out of the restaurant but still let them in the shop."

That was far more likely. Royce would deny it if asked, but Puck and Kirra had him wrapped around their paws. "Or that."

Clint grinned but sobered quickly. "Will you be okay if I leave next Monday? Mom's surgery isn't until Thursday, but I'd like a chance to get settled before I have to take her in."

"I can run this store without you, I promise. I've done it before."

"Not often. And usually with more warning than this."

That was true, but it wasn't like Royce was incapable of handling things. He was going to miss his friend more than his employee, especially if things progressed with Shawn. "I'll give Brandy and Lisa more hours or spend less time in the back and more time out here." That actually sounded nice. "Worry about your mother. I'll worry about the store."

Clint stepped out from behind the bar. "All right. I'll see you in a few weeks, then."

"Not now." Royce rolled his eyes. "I meant while you're gone. I still need you for the next week."

"Oh, fine," Clint said good-naturedly. "Go do paperwork. Kirra and I will hold down the fort."

"I'm a little afraid of what the two of you are going to get up to," Royce said, but he headed toward the coffee mug he'd left on the front counter anyway. If he got all the paperwork done now, he could call Shawn tonight. "Just make sure the place is still standing when I get back."

12

BY TWO forty-five on Saturday, Royce felt like he was going to lose his mind. The shop had been moderately busy all afternoon, enough that he'd stuck around to help Clint and Lisa instead of going to the office to take care of things back there, but not so busy he didn't have time to think. He spent the day wondering if three o'clock was early enough to leave and still get a proper tour of the vineyard before dark or if he should have told Shawn to come by earlier.

The bell above the door jingled several times as Royce rang people out. He looked over every time, hoping he'd see Shawn walk through door, and was disappointed every time to see it was just another customer.

"You should've gone to get him," Clint said when the line dwindled and they were both standing behind the counter with nothing to do for a few minutes. "You could have left already."

"I offered. He said that since I was driving out to the vineyard, the least he could do was meet me here." It also gave Shawn plausible deniability. If someone saw him or his car here, he could tell Henry he'd gone to buy wine. If someone saw Royce at Shawn's place, there would be nothing Shawn could say to make things okay with his boss.

"So, what? You think he's not coming, then?" Clint regarded Royce skeptically. "I doubt it, given how often you talked this week."

Royce shook his head. He'd talked to Shawn every night this week. Most of them had been just a few short text messages, but twice they'd spent close to an hour talking on the phone. He knew Shawn was coming. "I know. I'm just worried we'll be too late to really see Heartwood. I've talked it up enough I don't want him to be disappointed."

"Yes. I'm sure the vineyard is what he's really interested in. He's going to be crushed if he doesn't get to see all of it."

Royce scowled at Clint. He was convinced Clint had a personal sarcasm quota he needed to meet each day. "That's not the point. It doesn't matter why we're going. I still want him to get as much out of it as he can."

"As much out of what as who can?"

Royce grinned as he turned. He hadn't heard the door jingle again, but it must have, because Shawn was standing on the other side of the counter, grinning at him. "As much out of the vineyard tour as you can. I was wondering if we should have left earlier. We might not have time to see everything before it gets dark."

"If we don't, we'll just have to go back out there some other time." Shawn smiled easily and looked more relaxed than Royce had seen him since before their first date. "It'll give us another excuse to get out of town."

If getting out of Portland made Shawn smile like that, Royce didn't need any other excuse, but he would take one if Shawn offered it. "True. I'd still like you to see enough to know it's worth coming back, though."

"I'm sure it will be." Shawn glanced over his shoulder. "Are you ready to go, or do you need to take care of more here? I can wait if you're too busy to leave."

"I pay people for a reason. I was just keeping busy until you got here."

"He was just fretting, he means," Clint said. "Throwing customers at him was the best way to keep him relatively calm."

Royce thought about protesting, but Clint was right, and objecting would just emphasize that. Instead, he shook his head and stepped out from behind the counter. "I just need to grab my coat from upstairs. I'll be right back."

He hurried, afraid Shawn would realize any of the dozen or so customers on the shop could know Henry and report back to him, but he needn't have fretted. He came back down, coat and umbrella in hand, to find Shawn happily chatting with Clint and petting Puck. The cat was sitting on top of a stack of wine crates near the counter and accepting Shawn's attention like it was his due. Royce watched for a moment, amazed at the way Puck responded to Shawn's attention. "Trying to seduce my cat away from me?"

"If all it takes are a few pets, you're in trouble letting him wander around down here." Shawn scratched behind Puck's ears and grabbed a bag off the counter. "Anyone could catch his attention."

Royce laughed as he slipped his coat on. "He doesn't let most people pet him like that. He must like you." Puck wasn't shy, but he didn't usually relish attention from strangers, either. Usually, he'd let them get in one or two strokes and then he'd wander off. If they followed, he'd head back upstairs or jump up to the top shelf, where no one could reach him. A few regular customers were granted the privilege of his attention for more than a few seconds, but Royce had never seen him respond to anyone new like he had Shawn. Royce and Clint could pet him like that, but even Brandy, Lisa, and Jess didn't get that sort of acknowledgement from Puck.

"Huh." Shawn followed Royce out of the shop. "Wonder why."

"Clint would say it's because he's smarter than we are."

"Stasia would say that too." Shawn shrugged and climbed into the car. "Maybe he recognized my scent."

"Maybe." Royce personally thought it was far more likely Clint and Anastasia were right, but he kept that to himself. "Or he could have just been in a friendly mood today."

"Could be. What's his name, anyway? Clint didn't tell me and I've never seen him before. I thought you only had Kirra."

"Puck." Royce started the car and pulled out of the lot. "I've had him for five years. He probably came down to get away from Kirra, actually. She was zooming all over the place when I went upstairs."

Shawn laughed. "Kittens do that. He'll survive."

"I know. He actually likes her. Just don't tell him you know. It's a secret." Not a very closely kept one, granted, since Royce routinely found them curled up together, but occasionally Puck still liked to pretend Kirra was this interloper he couldn't stand.

"My lips are sealed." Shawn mimed zipping his lips and throwing away the key.

They rode in companionable silence for a while, and Royce's thoughts turned to the week ahead. He was mentally reviewing the arrangements he'd made to cover Clint's shifts for the third time when Shawn cleared his throat and caught Royce's attention. "Huh?"

"You okay? You seem... distracted." Shawn sounded concerned, but he also wasn't as open as he had been back in the shop, even though he had no reason to hide anything in the privacy of Royce's car.

"Yeah. Sorry." Royce glanced at Shawn and frowned. Shawn was sitting stiffly, his hands folded in his lap and his back ramrod straight, looking like he was there out of obligation, not desire. Royce had to fix this. "I, uh, have a lot on my mind."

"We don't have to do this now." The implied *or at all* sat heavily in the air.

"No! Sorry. I just…. Clint is leaving on Monday to go back to New York for a couple weeks. He sprung it on me Sunday, and I keep thinking I've forgotten something I need to take care of before he goes."

"Oh." Shawn relaxed a little. "Hasn't he taken time off before?"

"Of course. He usually doesn't tell me he'll be leaving in eight days and isn't sure when he'll be back."

"Oh." Shawn looked worried. "I hope everything's okay."

"Yeah." Royce smiled at Shawn's concern. "His mother is having surgery—nothing huge—and he's going to help her out. He thinks she'll need him for about two weeks, but he can't be sure. There's always the chance something could go wrong and she'll need him longer."

"And you're worried about the shop."

"No. I will be if he stays too long, but I can cover his shifts for a few weeks. Mostly, I'm worried about Clint. He doesn't go home very often." Clint had actually only gone home once in the almost eight years Royce had known him and it hadn't ended well. Royce had never heard what happened—it had been in the early stages of their friendship—but it had haunted Clint for weeks afterward, and he still clammed up every time Royce mentioned it. He hadn't connected the dots when Clint had asked about going home, but he'd worried about it ever since he remembered.

"I'm sure he wouldn't go if he didn't think things would be okay."

That wasn't true. Clint was the kind of guy who would do anything for the people he cared about. If his mother needed him, he'd be there no matter what. Royce couldn't tell Shawn that, though. He'd already said too much. "I hope."

"He will be," Shawn said firmly. "Now stop worrying."

Royce had been trying to do that all week, with little success, but Shawn managed to distract him by talking about the pranks Anastasia had played on the cruise. That led to Royce talking about Clint playing pranks on him, and Shawn telling stories about the shenanigans he and Anastasia had gotten up to in college. By the time they got to the vineyard, Royce was laughing so hard he could barely see to park.

"Spectacular job," Shawn said after he climbed out and looked at the car.

Royce had gotten it completely between the lines, but that was all that could be said for his parking job. The car was at an odd angle and close enough to the line on the driver's side that he could have trouble getting back in if someone was parked next to him when they were done. He thought about trying again, but there were plenty of free spaces in the lot and he didn't want to waste time worrying about how well he was parked. "You wish you could park this well."

Shawn laughed, still as carefree as he'd been in the car. "Yes. That's it exactly."

"I knew it. Maybe if you're lucky, I'll show you how when we're done here." Royce kept his tone light, but his heart pounded in his chest as he held out his hand. "Come on."

Shawn hesitated, then slowly took Royce's outstretched hand. It was awkward at first, their palms pressed together with their hands pointing perpendicular to each other, but then Shawn turned his hand and laced his fingers between Royce's. "Lead the way."

Royce's heart leaped in his chest like he was a giddy teenager holding hands with his crush for the first time, but he tried to keep his feelings from showing. This wasn't supposed to be a big deal, and if he reminded Shawn it was, he might remind Shawn *why* it was, and scare him away. Until Shawn made some sort of decision regarding Delicto, they'd never have a date completely free of the specter of Henry hanging over them, but Royce could minimize Henry's influence here by not bringing him up.

"Follow me," he said, keeping his fingers laced with Shawn's. He led the way into the main building, relishing the feel of Shawn's hand against his as they walked. Inside, he spotted the person he'd been hoping to see right away and headed over. "Drew! How are you?"

"Royce! Hey, man!" Drew set down the long case he was carrying and pulled Royce into an awkward one-armed hug. "I didn't expect to see you here this weekend. Thought you weren't coming by until next week!"

"I'm not here on business." Royce carefully extracted himself from the hug as he tried to figure out what to say next. He didn't want to say anything that would make it uncomfortable for Shawn, but he wasn't sure how else to explain why he was here.

"Pleasure, huh?" Drew looked down at their joined hands and winked. "I get it."

"This is Shawn, my date." It really was pointless to try to hide anything when they were holding hands. "Shawn, this is Drew. He works here."

"Only when I can't get out of it." Drew held his hand out to Shawn. "Nice to meetcha."

"Likewise." Shawn let go of Royce's hand long enough to shake Drew's. "What do you do around here?"

He didn't sound like he believed Drew actually worked at all, something Royce could easily understand. Drew didn't look like the rest of the people who worked at the vineyard, his long hair, ratty jeans, and layered T-shirts a sharp contrast to the business-casual look favored by the other employees. The workers in the production areas dressed more like Drew, but they weren't the people who usually interacted with the public.

"This and that." Drew shrugged and picked his case back up. "Whatever I can't get someone else to do."

"Drew's family owns Heartwood Vineyards," Royce explained since he knew Drew wouldn't. He'd met Drew several times before he finally realized that the Drew he kept running into on his visits was the Andrew who kept coming up in his meetings with Jonathan, the owner. It had taken him a while to put it together because Jonathan kept insisting he was grooming his son to take over the vineyard someday, and Royce couldn't imagine Drew taking over anything except a lounge chair. He'd since learned Drew was a very dedicated worker when he cared about something; he just resented his parents planning his future without giving him any choice.

"Ohhh." Shawn drew out the word.

Royce grinned, knowing Shawn understood. "You want to give us a tour, or are you sneaking off somewhere?" He looked pointedly at the case in Drew's hand. He'd never forget the first time he saw Drew shooting arrows down a row of grapes.

"I was heading out, but I can take you around." He glanced over at the counter, where most of the vineyard's other employees were gathered, helping customers. "You'll have to wait for someone else and none of them can give you the best tour anyway."

"Best tour?" Shawn looked skeptical again. "What's the best tour?"

"The one where I take you into all the back rooms and conveniently turn my back long enough for you to make out." Drew smirked. "No promises I don't peek, though."

"We're not putting on a private show for you." Royce would like nothing more than to hide in a back room with Shawn, but he wasn't into exhibitionism, and that included making out in front of Drew.

"Damn!" Drew snapped his fingers. "Well, it was worth a shot. Wait here while I go put this away, and I'll take you on Drew's Special Tour, sans make-out sessions. I'm warning you, though. It's not as much fun without the kissing."

"I think we'll manage," Royce said dryly.

"If you say so." Drew shook his head sadly. "Be right back. Don't move." He scurried off and disappeared through a door Royce knew led to the employee break area, and beyond it, the covered pathway to the family's house.

"So that's Drew," he said, more to full the silence than anything else.

"He's... interesting."

"Yeah. He's a good guy, though. He meant well when he offered to let us make out." Royce glanced down, gathered his courage, and looked back up at Shawn. "We could still take him up on the offer."

For an agonizing moment, Shawn was silent, and Royce started to wonder if he'd crossed some line. Maybe Shawn wasn't ready to risk more than they already were, even in the relative security of the winery's back rooms.

As Royce started to wonder if it was too late to pass it off as a joke, Shawn slowly smiled. "We could," he said, leaning in close to Royce's ear, "but I'd rather find someplace we can be completely alone."

13

HALFWAY through the tour, Shawn yanked Royce into one of the small storage rooms. Royce yelped and flailed, but Shawn had four inches in height and a few pounds of muscle on him, and ignored Royce's waving arm as he pushed him further into the room and shut the door.

"What are you doing?" Royce hissed as he stalked over to Shawn and tried to reach around him and grab the doorknob. "Drew will—"

"Think we're making out? I hope so. It was his idea."

Royce stared at him for a moment. "Who are you and what have you done with Shawn?"

"Nothing." Shawn smirked. "I just thought Drew was asking for us to disappear for a few minutes. He did keep pointing out the storage rooms, after all."

"And that's it? We're just playing a trick on Drew?" Royce took a step back. "Nothing else?"

The hint of disappointment in Royce's voice cut through Shawn. He'd planned to just play a little joke on Drew, who seemed like the kind of guy who would appreciate it, but they were the only people in the room, and only Drew knew they were back here. Even if one of Henry's friends happened to be at Heartwood Vineyards today and happened to see them in the restaurant later, he was safe now. No one but he and Royce would know what happened in this room. "Not just playing a joke."

He leaned in slowly, giving Royce ample time to read his intentions and step back. Instead, Royce leaned in and tipped his head back, angling his lips perfectly for Shawn to brush his against them. The first touch was startling. Shawn had been telling himself for weeks that he couldn't have, couldn't touch, couldn't look, so he wasn't prepared for the warmth of Royce's mouth under his. It felt hedonistic and dangerous, but that just made Shawn want it more. If they were doomed to be caught at any moment, he wanted to make the most of it.

He deepened the kiss, leaned in further and put his hands on Royce's shoulders. It was everything he remembered from that fleeting kiss after their first date and so much more, enhanced by the danger of being caught and the growing attraction between them. Shawn could easily lose himself in Royce's touch and let this turn into more, but the safety of the storeroom was mostly an illusion, and they weren't teenagers desperate to make out in any dark corner they could find.

He stepped back reluctantly. "It's no fun pretending to make out without a little kissing."

"That was a little?" Royce was flushed, his chest heaving with each breath, his lips pink and moist.

Shawn desperately wanted to kiss him again, the danger of being caught and the eighteen years that had passed since he was a teenager be damned. "Compared to what we should have done by now," he said as he leaned in.

The door opened just as their lips touched, and Shawn jerked back instinctively. He whirled around and pressed his hand to his chest, trying to calm the rapid thudding of his heart. "Drew! You scared me!"

"Damn! I missed it." Drew looked at them expectantly, but Shawn just looked right back at him, his expression as bland as he could make it considering the flush he felt in his cheeks and the way he couldn't catch his breath. Drew's hopeful expression gradually faded under the weight of Shawn's stare, and after a moment, he sighed. "Fine. We'd better get moving, anyway, or you'll miss dinner."

Right then, Shawn would rather have stayed in the supply room and kissed Royce, but his stomach had other ideas and rumbled as soon as Drew mentioned food. "Wouldn't want that." He held his hand out toward Royce, feeling brave enough to initiate it this time, and smiled as Royce laced their fingers together.

"I don't really like him right now," Royce muttered as he fell into step next to Shawn.

"Me either, but we'll pick this up later."

"I'm going to hold you to that."

Shawn knew Royce would, possibly even someplace that wasn't as remote as Heartwood Vineyards, and he found he was looking forward to it. Part of the thrill of making out in the storage room had been the chance they'd get caught. Shawn wasn't ready to do something drastic like kiss Royce in front of Henry, but if sneaking around felt like this instead of the awkward dance that had characterized their trip to the Portland Underground, he wanted more. He couldn't do everything he wanted yet, but maybe he didn't have to be quite so paranoid about Henry.

He smiled and waited until Royce was looking at him so it would be clear he meant it. "I know. I want you to."

Drew finished the tour of the vineyard before leading them to the restaurant, but Shawn honestly didn't pay attention to much of what Drew said. He focused on Royce instead, relishing the feel of their palms pressed together and the way their arms brushed as they walked. Most of all, he focused on how nice it was to hold Royce's hand without worrying about what anyone else thought. It was a liberating feeling, and he was a little sad when the tour was over, because eating meant he had to let go.

Drew led them all the way to the restaurant. "This is where I leave you," he said, rocking back on his heels. "Got things to do, people to hide from. You know the drill."

Royce laughed. "Take care."

"I'll see you next week, right?" When Royce nodded, Drew turned to Shawn. "Don't be a stranger, you hear? I expect Royce to bring you back sometime. He spends too much time working and not enough having fun."

Royce protested, but Drew ignored him and left with a jaunty wave over his shoulder. Shawn watched him leave and then turned to Royce. "I like him."

"He has a certain charm." Royce gestured to the restaurant. "Shall we?"

Shawn followed him inside and they let the hostess lead them to a table near the back. "This is nice," he said once they were seated.

The restaurant had a comfortable atmosphere, with a fireplace along one wall surrounded by groupings of easy chairs and coffee tables. The dining tables were a little fancier, covered with linen tablecloths and surrounded by fabric-covered chairs, but it wasn't so fancy Shawn felt out of place in his jeans. The lights were dim, but not to the point it was difficult to see, and candles flickered on each occupied table. The overall effect was welcoming, but with enough pizzazz to make it feel like a special occasion.

"Yeah." Royce picked up the menu and glanced at it. "They use locally sustainable products and specialize in pairing their wines with each dish. Sometimes it's not what you expect, but I've never had anything here that wasn't delicious."

"You eat here a lot?" It was a nice place, and Shawn could see why Royce liked it, but it wasn't the kind of restaurant most people would frequent for casual meals.

"When I come down for business. We usually have lunch or dinner meetings. It'll be odd picking my own food, actually. Jonathan usually has the chef make something special to accent whatever wine he's trying to sell me."

Shawn laughed. "So, do you have any idea what's good on the menu or are you as clueless as I am?"

Royce peered at the menu for a moment, then set it down and shook his head. "All of it, I'd guess, but I haven't had anything they're offering today. In my defense, they use what's fresh and available, so the menu changes daily. I could have ordered off the menu a dozen times and still not had any of this."

"Excuses, excuses." Shawn picked up his menu and started reading it. The list of food offered was short but diverse, with vegetarian options as well as local fish and game. Each entree had between one and three suggested wines listed next to it, and Shawn paid as much attention to those as he did to the food.

He'd narrowed it down to two options when a bottle of wine arrived at the table. "Compliments of Mr. Heartwood," the sommelier said as he presented the bottle and poured a taste.

"Drew?" Shawn asked.

"Or his father." Royce took a sip and nodded for the sommelier to go ahead and pour. "Very nice. Thank you. Jonathan wouldn't be above sending out a bottle he wants me to stock if he heard I was here."

The attached note answered the question quickly. *Thanks for the show. If you ever want to give me more than a preview, I'd be happy to hook you up with another back room. BTW, you won't find this one listed on our menu yet—we're not quite ready to share it with the world—so I recommend either the spinach pizza or the shepherd's pie. Try it. You won't be disappointed.—Drew*

Shawn handed the note back to Royce with a raised eyebrow. "I'm not giving him more than a preview."

"He doesn't really expect it." Royce tossed the note on the table and gestured to Shawn's glass. "You should try the wine, though. It's good."

Shawn took a sip. The wine was good, but even better was the look on Royce's face as he took a sip, the way their knees brushed together under the table, and the way Royce smiled as he set down his glass. Whatever the food tasted like, dinner was going to be good.

DINNER was fantastic, the wine even more so, and by the end of the night Shawn was feeling slightly tipsy and more than slightly giddy. He hooked his arm in Royce's as they walked out to the car, relishing the chance to touch him without worrying about who might see. When they got to the parking lot, he reluctantly let go to let Royce walk around to the other side of the car, then climbed in as quickly as he could, anxious to regain contact while he still could.

After Royce climbed into the car, Shawn reached for him, intending to take his hand. At the last moment, he decided to take advantage of the dark parking lot while he could and instead grabbed Royce's shoulder and pulled him in for a kiss.

They were both too big and too old to make out in a car like horny teenagers, but Shawn's libido didn't get the message. He moaned into Royce's mouth and squirmed in his seat as he tried to get more contact. The center console was inconvenient, the confined space even more so. He longed to press his body against Royce's the way he hadn't dared in the stockroom, but all he could do was hold Royce's shoulders and wish for more.

By the time they broke apart, Shawn was panting heavily and his hardening cock tented his pants. He shifted, trying to relieve the pressure without drawing attention to it, but Royce noticed and smirked as he reached over. "Can I?"

Shawn nodded, still swept up in the surge of desire that had pushed him to kiss Royce in the first place. He didn't know what Royce intended, but it didn't matter. Right now he wanted whatever Royce was offering, and he felt safe enough to give in.

Royce slid his hand over Shawn's groin, pressing just hard enough to make his cock jump to attention. It was straining the fabric of his jeans now, more uncomfortable than pleasurable, but he didn't want Royce to stop. "Please."

"We shouldn't," Royce said, withdrawing his hand. "Someone could see."

Shawn moaned at the loss and cursed Royce's caution. It was dark out, and the dome light in the car had turned off while they were kissing. The lights in the parking lot glowed brightly enough Shawn could see the flush on Royce's cheeks and the tent in his pants, but it was unlikely anyone would notice them in a dark car in the dark lot.

He said as much, then leaned in, put his hand on Royce's cock, and kissed him again. If they'd been somewhere else, he would have rubbed their bodies together until they both came, but he had to settle for pushing his palm against Royce's erection and kissing him deeply.

Royce moaned and kissed Shawn back, but he pulled away too soon and gently removed Shawn's hand from his crotch. "We can't." He sounded genuinely regretful. "Henry."

The mention of Shawn's boss dampened his desire a little but he pushed the thought aside and focused on Royce. He looked delectable, his face flushed, his lips moist and parted, his pupils wide. "Henry isn't here and I don't want to think about him."

"The Heartwoods, then." Royce stopped Shawn from leaning in again. "They're business associates. I can't get a hand job in their parking lot!"

Shawn nodded. He didn't like it, but he couldn't object, especially since Royce was putting up with so much because of *his* business aspirations. "Okay." He folded his hands in his lap so Royce could see he wasn't reaching for anything. "Can I just…?" He leaned in, and when Royce nodded, Shawn kissed him again.

He tried to keep this kiss soft and short, but Royce had other ideas. He held Shawn in place with one hand at the back of his neck, pushed his tongue into Shawn's mouth, and proceeded to take Shawn apart with nothing more than a kiss.

When Royce pulled away, Shawn cursed and thunked his head against the headrest. "Fuck. We're acting like horny teenagers."

"I never did anything like this as a teenager. I didn't know how."

The thought of Royce learning how to kiss like that was more than Shawn could handle, and he moaned as he pressed his palm against his crotch. "You can't say things like that and expect me to stop."

"Sorry." Royce took a deep breath and let it out slowly. "We really should stop while we still can."

"Yeah." Shawn was past that point, but he thought about Henry and his grandmother and the bugs they'd cleaned out of the kitchen on the last *Restaurant: Impossible* and his erection started to subside. A glance at Royce as he started the car was enough to bring it back, though. He bit his lip as Royce pulled out of the lot. It was going to be a long drive home.

14

WHEN Shawn got home from work the next day, he planned to heat up a frozen dinner, down a beer or two while he ate, and crawl into bed so he could fantasize about taking things further with Royce and forget every minute he'd spent at Delicto. Instead, he found Anastasia on his couch and what smelled like lasagna in his oven. "Doesn't the Navy have things for you to do?"

"Hello, Shawn," she said, peering at him over the top of her book. "It's good to see you too. I'm great, thanks for asking. Yes, I did cook dinner. Glad you noticed. I was tired of commissary food, and I thought you might want a break from Delicto and frozen meals. I figured we could catch up and you could tell me how your date went."

He didn't leave the apartment, but he did walk back over to the door, open it, and shut it again. "Stasia!" he said with far more enthusiasm than he ever used. "How are you? How'd you get time off to come down? Do I smell something cooking?"

Anastasia lowered her book again. Her expression hadn't changed much, but her eyes were twinkling and Shawn could tell she was fighting a smile. "You're ridiculous," she said flatly, and then she gave in and grinned.

"I try." Shawn plucked the book from Anastasia's hand, set it aside, and pulled her into a hug. "Sorry. I am glad to see you. It's just been a bad day."

"Henry?" Anastasia patted Shawn's arm as she extracted herself and sat back down. All traces of her earlier teasing were gone, wiped away by her concern. "Is he still giving you trouble?"

"Some." Shawn flopped on the couch and closed his eyes. "It was just one of those days, you know? I woke up in a bad mood and everything went down from there. People were late, people called in sick, things broke, orders got messed up... and the whole time Henry was there, judging me. It didn't matter how I handled it, I felt like he didn't like it. And then he started talking about how he'd had other people talk to him about buying the restaurant." He sighed, trying to let go of some of his irritation, but it pressed down on him like a lead weight. "He didn't say it, but I felt like he was wondering why he should sell to me when he had other offers and I couldn't even run the place anymore."

"He has *offers*?" Anastasia leaned in close. "Actual offers or people who have expressed an interest in buying it?"

"I don't know." Shawn rubbed his hand over his face and leaned forward. "He hasn't really talked to me about it, just mentioned it in passing." That was the most frustrating thing. The last time someone had approached Henry about buying Delicto, he'd sat down with Shawn to seriously discuss the option. Then, he'd needed to know how serious Shawn was, because he'd been willing to wait until Shawn could manage financially as long as he had a plan in place and was diligently saving. Now Shawn had almost the entire down payment saved up, and Henry hadn't even asked if he was still interested.

"Okay. Well, I guess you need to decide if you really still want to buy the place after everything Henry's put you through. And if you do, make a formal offer. If he agrees, you can take it to the bank to get financing."

"I don't have a full down payment yet. I'm still a couple thousand short."

"So I'll give it to you," Anastasia said. Then, because she knew he would never take that kind of money as a gift, she corrected herself. "Lend it to you but tell the bank it was a present. Whatever."

"And if I don't want to buy Delicto anymore?" The thought had crossed his mind several times over the past four months, but this was the first time he'd said it out loud. It was terrifying, and he was surprised his voice didn't shake. "What then?"

"You tell Henry to go fuck himself."

"Stasia!" Shawn gaped at her. The idea was admittedly tempting, especially with Henry acting the way he had today, but it wasn't something he could let himself think about. "I can't just—"

"Yes, you can. He deserves it." Anastasia turned to sit sideways on the couch and put her hand over Shawn's. "Seriously, he treats you like crap. If you really want to buy Delicto, and you think it's worth putting up with him, then fine. I'll support you. You know that. But if owning Delicto isn't worth putting up with him, why are you still there?"

"Because I haven't decided." Shawn flipped his hand over and squeezed Anastasia's as he thought about how to explain this to her. She saw it in black and white—Henry was hurting him and there was nothing else to consider—but it was more complicated for Shawn. He had history with Delicto and with Henry, and though Henry was being unfair now, he'd given Shawn a lot over the years, and Shawn wasn't ready to just let that go. "I know Henry isn't being great right now, but he's not a bad person. He's just a product of his time. He cares about Delicto and everyone who works there."

"You need to stop making excuses for him."

"I'm not."

"Yes, you are!" Anastasia jerked her hand back and squeezed it into a fist as she glared at Shawn. "You're so used to the idea that you can't change Henry's mind that you don't even think you should try. It isn't okay."

"He has every right to—"

"No, he doesn't!" Anastasia ran a hand through her hair and took a deep breath. She was clearly far more upset than Shawn was about the whole thing, even though he was the one who had to deal with Henry five days a week. "He has the right to decide not to sell to you, yes, but that's it. He doesn't have the right to treat you like crap, and you can't tell me he cares about everyone who works for him right now. He doesn't seem to care about you."

"He does. He just—" Shawn didn't get the chance to elaborate. Anastasia interrupted him with enough vehemence he leaned back, afraid of what she would do next. She was trained in combat, and he had no doubt she could take him down despite being much smaller than he was.

"He doesn't *just* anything! He's. Not. Being. Fair. To. You." The last time Shawn had seen Anastasia this upset was in college, right after they'd realized they made much better friends than lovers, and someone they'd thought was a mutual friend had tried to use that to hurt them both. Anastasia had punched the guy then, and Shawn had no doubt she wanted to do the same to Henry now.

"Stasia," he said, trying to calm her down. It didn't work.

"Don't 'Stasia' me!" Anastasia snapped, and then she visibly calmed herself. "You have to get out of there, Shawn," she said earnestly. "Buy the place or quit, I don't care, but I won't let you keep doing this to yourself. It's not okay for Henry to treat you like this, and I can't let you think it is."

Shawn hadn't heard her use that tone since she'd convinced him to come out to his parents, and it scared him a little to hear it now. Things were bad with Henry, yes, but he didn't think they were *that* bad. "What am I going to do if I quit?" He knew what he'd do if he bought the place, though he wasn't sure he was ready for that yet.

He thought he had a few more months to save, a few more months to adjust to the idea of making his dream a reality, and the idea of it happening sooner was both elating and terrifying.

"Date Royce." Anastasia smiled softly at Shawn's unimpressed look. She knew what he meant and that wasn't it. "Get another job somewhere else. Sell your art. Buy a different restaurant."

"Restaurants aren't just available on a store shelf," Shawn muttered. Anastasia's ideas were fine, but it wasn't like he could just go make an offer on any restaurant he wanted and get it. Even if he could find another restaurant he wanted to buy and convince the owner to sell, it wouldn't be an immediate process, and he'd have to have some income until then. Buying Delicto meant he could keep being Henry's employee right up until he took ownership, and there wouldn't be any gap in his income. Anything else would be more complicated.

"I know. That doesn't mean you can't keep an eye out for one. Meanwhile, you keep dating Royce and get another job somewhere you won't be treated like crap. Or you go ahead and make an offer on Delicto and make Henry decide."

"Jobs aren't exactly plentiful right now, either, Stasia." He held up his hand to stop Anastasia from protesting. "I'll think about it, okay? But I'm not going to walk in there for my next shift and either quit or buy the place. I have to decide what I want, and if I don't buy Delicto, I have to find something else to do *before* I quit." It was still hard to think about not buying it, but he had to make his point.

"As long as you think about it." Anastasia sat back, apparently satisfied. "You can supplement whatever else you do with your art if you quit, you know."

"No, I can't." Shawn hardly showed his original stuff to anyone, and he couldn't sell the fan art. "No one will want to buy it."

"Yes, they will. You just have to get people to see it."

"People have seen it." Not enough people to build an audience, but people. "You're the only person I'm not related to who wants any of my original art."

"I'm the only person you're not related to who you've *shown* most of your original art to," Anastasia said dryly. "Adding a thumbnail here and there around your fan art does not count as showing off your original stuff."

That was exactly how Shawn wanted it. If people didn't like his fan art, that was fine. They were just doodles that didn't mean much to him. But he knew from experience how mean people could be, and he wasn't ready to expose the pieces he'd put his heart and soul into to that kind of criticism. "I know." He kept his tone deliberately light, though it was unlikely Anastasia would miss his sudden nervousness at the idea. "I don't want people to know about it. No one would want to buy it anyway."

"Not true." Anastasia poked Shawn in the chest. "I know at least one person who does. And I'm sure there would be more if you just put your art out there."

"Who?" Shawn batted her hand away. "And how did they see anything I've done?"

"Wooton. He helped me hang the painting you gave me for my birthday last year, and he asked who did it. I told him you did, and he wanted to know if you took commissions or if you had anything you'd be willing to sell." She looked at him seriously. "You should think about it. Even if you don't leave Delicto, it would be cool to make money for painting and drawing."

"My mother would approve," Shawn said dryly. That was the only plus he could see in the idea, though. He needed to draw and paint the same way he needed to eat and sleep, but the idea of letting someone else dictate what he created felt no better than letting Henry dictate his personal life.

"She would, but that's not why you should do it."

"Why should I do it, then?" Shawn had no doubt Anastasia thought he should do this, at least for her friend. She wouldn't have brought it up otherwise.

"Because it'll be good for you." Anastasia sighed as Shawn regarded her dubiously. "Will you at least think about doing something for Wooton? As a test. For me. If you hate it, I promise, I'll never bring it up again."

"And if I don't hate it, you'll keep pushing me until I start selling more?" He knew how she worked.

"Only if you actually like it. I promise," Anastasia said, though Shawn was sure that if he showed the slightest hint of interest in any other commissions, she wouldn't let go of the idea until he agreed.

"I'll think about it."

The look she gave him could only be described as pleading. "I'll make it worth your while."

Anything she'd offer him was something he could convince her to do anyway, and they both knew it. They both knew he'd most likely agree to do something for Wooton, too, just because she was asking, but he did actually need to think about it. If he decided to move on buying Delicto, he wouldn't have time.

"I'm sure you will," he said dryly. "I promise, I'll think about it and let you know soon. All right?"

"Fine." Anastasia was silent for a moment. Then she leaned over and bumped her shoulder against Shawn's. "So, how was your date?"

"Oh God." Shawn groaned and buried his head in his hands. "Don't ask."

"Yeah. Right. Like I'm going to let it go after you react like *that*." Anastasia pulled her legs up, crossed them, and looked at Shawn attentively. "Now, come on. Tell me what happened. I'm not going to believe you if you tell me it was bad."

Shawn sighed as he straightened. "It wasn't bad. It was nice, actually. Really nice. We went on a tour of one of the wineries he buys from and... I kissed him." He grinned as he remembered that kiss in the back room. It had been almost chaste compared to what they'd done later, but the memory warmed him from the inside out, and if he could keep one moment of the night on an endless loop, it would be that.

"In front of people?" Anastasia sounded incredulous, but she was grinning almost as widely as Shawn, and he knew she was happy for him.

"Not really. It was a private tour, just the two of us and the owner's son. Drew kept teasing us about good spots to make out, so I pulled Royce into one halfway through the tour." Shawn mentally replayed the kiss again, focusing on the softness of Royce's lips beneath his and the thrill of danger and daring that had permeated the air. "Drew came in right at the end, but we were alone for most of it."

"And?"

"And it was awesome and I'm not telling you anything else." He smirked at Anastasia. "You don't need to know."

"You're wrong about that, but I'll let it slide this time." Anastasia waved her hand, magnanimously forgiving Shawn for the imagined slight. "But if that part was awesome, what made you groan when I asked about your date? Did dinner suck? Did you see someone? I'd ask if Royce was secretly an asshole, but I don't think you'd be grinning about the kiss like that if he was."

"No, he's not secretly an asshole." Shawn laughed at the thought. He'd use a lot of words to describe Royce—thoughtful, smart, charming, really hot, *incredibly* patient—but asshole wasn't one of them. "And dinner was fine. Delicious, actually. Drew sent out a bottle of wine they weren't selling yet, and I had this incredible spinach pizza to go with it. And chocolate cake for dessert."

"So after dinner, then?" Anastasia looked at him shrewdly for a moment, then brightened and sat up straighter. "Did you have sex? Tell me you had sex and you're going to share all the details."

"No!" Shawn buried his face in his hands again. "I did not have sex. And you wouldn't get details if I did."

"I believe the second, but not so much the first." Anastasia pulled Shawn's hands away from his face. "Something happened. Now tell."

"I kissed him in the car afterward, and then—" Shawn groaned, thinking about it. Anastasia was never going to let him live this down. "God, Stasia, we were like teenagers. I don't remember who grabbed who first, but we started feeling each other up, and I wanted to climb into his lap or pull him into the backseat. We almost had sex in the parking lot!"

As he'd expected, Anastasia cracked up. She doubled over as she laughed, clutching her stomach and gasping for breath. "You? Mr. I Can't Do Anything That Might Get Back To Henry? Really?"

"Yes!" Shawn was sure he was the color of a ripe tomato by now. He could feel his face burning with embarrassment, and it just got worse as he thought about it. He remembered sliding his hand over Royce's groin and Royce sliding his tongue into his mouth and suddenly, it wasn't just embarrassment heating up his face. "I was caught up in the moment, okay? It was supposed to be one last kiss while we were safe from prying eyes, and I was a little tipsy and...." He shrugged.

"And you really like him." Anastasia smiled and nodded as though she'd just decided something. "Good. I like him too. You should keep seeing him."

"I'm so glad I have your approval," Shawn said dryly, though he knew if Anastasia had decided she didn't like Royce, he would have started second-guessing his feelings. "It makes me feel *so* much better."

"It should," she said, and she stood. "Now, come on. Lasagna should be almost ready and you didn't give me any real details. Go change while I finish cooking and then you're going to tell me *everything* that happened last night."

Shawn wanted to think he'd keep some of the details to himself, but he knew better than to argue. Instead, he stared at her for a moment, then rolled his eyes and stood. "Yes, dear." Anastasia's annoyed look was worth whatever payback she'd come up with later.

15

PAYBACK came in the form of getting dragged to another wine tasting at All Corked Up—hardly a punishment until Shawn realized Anastasia intended to use the opportunity to get Royce on her side about the commission for Wooton. He tried to drag her out the door as soon as it clicked, but Royce had already seen them and waved them over with a smile that made Anastasia smirk.

"I told you I'd get you to agree," she said as they headed over to the counter.

"And I told you I'd think about it!" Shawn hissed in a low voice that did little to hide his irritation. "That means you have to give me time to think."

Anastasia stopped and looked at him with a distinctly unimpressed expression on her face. "Don't tell me you're not happy to be here. I know you want to see Royce."

"I do," Shawn agreed easily. He almost always wanted to see Royce these days. What he didn't want was for Anastasia to meddle. She meant well, he knew, and she only had his best interests at heart, but sometimes she could be a little much. "I don't want you two to gang up on me about doing something for Wooton, though."

He held Anastasia's gaze for a long moment before she deflated and nodded. "All right. No ganging up on you, I promise."

"And no pushing me at Royce, either," he added, sure that making up for Saturday had been her secondary goal. "We're perfectly capable of deciding for ourselves what we want… and we *have been.*"

Anastasia pouted a little at that, but she nodded. "All right. No making the two of you hook up. Am I at least allowed to imply I won't be heartbroken if I go home alone tonight?"

Shawn hooked his arm through hers. "*If* it comes up."

Anastasia rolled her eyes as she let Shawn guide her toward the counter. "You're no fun. It's a damn good thing I'm not trying to live vicariously through you. I'd go nuts waiting."

"Yes, because your love life is so much more active than mine. When was the last time you had a date again? A year ago?"

"Yes, but I don't want a relationship right now." Anastasia grinned wickedly as she stretched up on her toes and tugged Shawn down so she was as close to his ear as possible. "*I'm* perfectly happy with my vibrator. I don't need a man."

Shawn blushed so hard he could have doubled as a stop sign. "Stasia! You shouldn't…! I don't…!" She patted his arm in a way that would have made him glare if he hadn't been completely distracted by images of Anastasia naked. He hadn't pictured her that way since they broke up and he certainly didn't want to think about it now. "Don't say things like that!"

"Try and stop me." She slipped her arm out of his as they stepped up to the counter. "Hey, Royce."

Royce looked amused as he glanced between Shawn and Anastasia. "I don't think I want to know."

"You don't," Shawn said fervently. "Trust me."

Anastasia laughed. "I'm just traumatizing Shawn. Don't worry, I don't know you well enough to traumatize you yet."

"*Yet.* That's comforting." Royce eyed her dubiously, but he didn't look like the idea was completely unappealing.

Shawn nudged Anastasia to stop her from saying anything else. "She's just upset because I won't let her meddle and that's her favorite thing."

"One of them, anyway." Anastasia beamed. "And how are you, Royce?"

"Okay." For a minute, Royce looked like he wanted to say something else, but then he shrugged, grabbed two wine glasses, and passed them across the counter. "Lisa! Come take over the front, would you?" When she got there, he grabbed another wine glass and walked around the counter to join Shawn and Anastasia.

It looked like he was going to join them, which delighted Shawn to no end, but he couldn't help the little niggle of worry that wormed its way into his thoughts. "Don't you have to work?"

"Not at the moment. It's a small tasting, which is good since I'm down a person, so I thought I'd join you." He led the way into the back room, where Jess was working the tasting bar. "I can't promise I won't be needed at some point tonight, but for now, as long as I'm here to keep an eye on things, that's enough."

"Perfect." Anastasia hooked her arms through both of theirs and steered them to the back room. "So what's the best wine tonight?"

"Whichever one you like the best." Royce laughed at Anastasia's gobsmacked expression. "Seriously. It's different for everyone. The best wine tonight for you is the one you enjoy the most. That's all that matters, really."

Anastasia looked calculatingly at Royce. "I can't tell if you're putting on a sales pitch or if you actually believe that."

"He believes it," Shawn said as they stopped in the short line at the counter. "And it makes sense, if you think about it. We don't all like the same food, why should we all like the same wine?"

"Besides, if I were making a sales pitch, I'd try to convince you the most expensive wine was the best," Royce added dryly. He held out his glass as they reached the counter. "The first one, please, Jess. For all of us."

"Slacking off, boss?" she asked as she poured about an ounce of wine into each of their glasses.

Royce swirled the glass under his nose and sniffed it delicately. "Just enjoying myself. I'm here if you need me, though I'm confident you ladies can handle it with this crowd."

"We can handle it with a lot bigger crowd than this, boss. Go have fun."

Shawn followed as Royce led them into a corner and turned so they formed a triangle with each of them facing the center. It was a small area, and his shoulder brushed against Royce's as he sipped his wine. It was nice and perfectly innocuous to an outside viewer—his shoulder was almost brushing Anastasia's as well—so Shawn let himself feel a little thrill every time he and Royce touched.

"So," Shawn said, drawing out the word as he tried to think of anything to say. There were things he wanted to talk about with Royce, but not with Anastasia here, and things he could talk about with Anastasia, but they'd exclude Royce. He was usually good at this sort of small talk—he used it all the time at Delicto—but tonight his skills had abandoned him.

"Wine's nice," Anastasia said, taking another sip. "I usually prefer reds, but this isn't bad for a white."

"It has its uses," Royce agreed. "Clint really likes this one with spicy stuff. I prefer the Mercer Riesling, but this one works too."

"How is Clint, by the way?" Shawn desperately grasped on to the topic in the hope that it would at least keep them talking until they were ready for the next wine. "Did he get to his mother's okay? Has she has her surgery yet?"

"She had it yesterday. Clint texted me when he got there and to let me know the surgery went well, but I haven't really talked to him since he left. I think he's bonding with his mother. He doesn't see her very often."

Shawn could see how off-kilter Royce felt with Clint gone, and he frowned. He understood the feeling well from when Anastasia was on cruise, and he hated that Royce was feeling it. "How much longer is he staying there?"

Royce finished his wine with one long swallow. "At least another week. Maybe more, depending on how things go. I told him to just keep me updated and not to worry about how long he was gone." He held his glass above his mouth and shook the last few drops down his throat. "Come on, let's go get more."

Shawn still had a couple of swallows left in his glass, but he drank them as he followed Royce back to the counter. Jess poured the second wine into each of their glasses, but the line had picked up a little by then, so they quickly moved away from the counter to let her serve the next customer. Royce frowned at the line when they stopped in the corner again. "I think everyone wanted another pour at once." He watched Jess for a second, then handed his glass to Shawn. "Hold that, would you? I'm going to help Jess get caught up. Be right back."

Anastasia nudged Shawn as soon as Royce was gone. "Are you that thrown off when I go on cruise?"

Shawn glared at her. She was far too gleeful about that possibility. "No. I'm used to you being unreachable for months at a time. And I don't *need* to see you every few days to function."

"Uh-huh. Keep telling yourself that." Anastasia patted his arm. "Were you that thrown off the first time I went on cruise?"

"No." He'd learned to cope by the time she'd gone in her first cruise. Basic and A-school, though, had been a different story.

Shawn was still convinced that stretch had been harder on him than it had been on her parents. "I do know how to manage without you."

"I'd pay good money to see that."

"See what?" Royce asked as he took his wine back from Shawn.

Shawn let his fingers brush against Royce's as he handed over the glass. "She thinks I'm incapable of coping without her. I think she's confusing missing her with needing her around."

"He seemed to be coping just fine when I met him."

"You distracted him. Besides, you didn't have something to compare it to. You're not an accurate judge." Anastasia smirked and took a sip of her wine. Her expression faltered as she swallowed. "Wow. That's, uh…."

Shawn took a sip of his wine and forced himself to swallow. If it wouldn't have drawn too much attention, he would have legitimately spit it out. "Yeah. Okay. I don't think I'll be buying this one." He frowned as Royce calmly sipped from his glass. "Do you really like it?"

"It's not my favorite of the night, but it's all right." Royce shrugged and headed back toward the counter. He dumped his glass into the spittoon and held out his hand for Shawn's. "I'd usually recommend trying it with food to see how that changes the flavor, but if you dislike it that much, food probably isn't going to save it for you."

"Probably not." Shawn took his glass back after Jess poured the next wine into it and sniffed it. "I hope this one is better."

Royce finished dumping Anastasia's glass and passed it over to Jess. "Based on what you've enjoyed in the past, I think you'll like it."

It smelled better, anyway. The last wine had cloyingly sweet smell that overwhelmed Shawn's nostrils when he sipped it, but this one smelled crisp and refreshing. "I'd better, or I'm going to stop coming to these tastings."

The look on Royce's face made it clear he didn't believe Shawn meant that at all. "Oh no," he deadpanned, putting his hand over his heart but not changing his expression. "Whatever shall I do?"

Anastasia slung her arm over Royce's shoulder. "I can give you some ideas, if you want to torment him. I'm good at that."

"Nah." Royce laughed as he slipped free of Anastasia's grip and bumped his shoulder against Shawn's. "I think I'll just have him make it up to me."

Well, if that was what he wanted.... "I'm sure I can think of a way to do that." Shawn glanced around the room and leaned in so his lips were right by Royce's ear. "I can start now, if you want to get away for a few minutes."

"Want to, absolutely. Can...." Royce sighed melodramatically. "I really can't until the tasting is over."

Even though Shawn knew Royce was right, he took that as a personal challenge. "I bet I can change your mind."

SHAWN teased Royce the rest of the night, implying they should leave the tasting for other pursuits as often as he could without being obnoxious. By the time the tasting was over, Royce had developed a standard response that made Anastasia giggle every time he used it and Shawn had started asking just to hear the exaggerated southern accent he answered with.

At the end of the night, when Shawn and Anastasia were the only nonemployees left in the shop, Shawn leaned against the counter and looked at Royce. "You ready to take me upstairs so I can start apologizing for doubting your ability to pick wine?" Aside from the one he'd hated, Shawn's opinion of the wines had ranged from decent to amazing, and he'd picked up a couple bottles of the seventh one to take to his next family dinner.

Shawn had expected Royce to agree easily now that the tasting was over, but instead Royce shuffled his feet and looked around nervously. "Didn't Stasia ride with you?"

"I drove, and I'm perfectly capable of getting home all by myself," Anastasia said in a tone that dared Royce to imply she couldn't. "I don't need Shawn to escort me."

Royce held up his hands in a gesture of surrender. Whatever had changed his mood from flirtatious to nervous hadn't made him dumb enough to truly piss off Anastasia. "I just didn't want you stranded if Shawn had driven."

"Nope. We took my car. And you're close enough to the MAX that he can get himself home later."

"It's almost like you planned on leaving without me," Shawn said dryly. "Imagine that."

"I just arranged it so it was possible," Anastasia said innocently. It was amazing how well she could pull off the look even when Shawn knew she'd been plotting. "But you boys do need to make up your minds. Am I leaving alone, or with Shawn?"

Shawn shrugged and looked at Royce. "I'd like to stay, but it's up to you," he said quietly. There was little chance Anastasia couldn't hear them, but he didn't have to speak in a way that would include her in the conversation. "We have a few hours before I'd have to leave. It's still early."

Royce looked from Shawn to Anastasia and back again. "If you're sure it's okay," he said, directing his gaze somewhere between them.

"Positive," Anastasia said quickly. "I didn't want to assume Shawn would stay, but I did plan for the possibility. I'm okay going home alone."

Shawn had also planned for the possibility, but something about the way Royce was hesitating made him wonder if it was the best idea. "It's fine with me," he said, looking at Royce carefully, "but don't feel like you have to invite me up. I can go home just as easily."

"No." Royce shook his head and smiled. It wasn't his usual welcoming smile, but it didn't look too forced, either. "I'd like you to stay. I just didn't want to push the issue. I wasn't sure you'd be comfortable."

There was more to it than that, Shawn could tell, but the only way he was going to find out was to follow Royce upstairs. "There's no one here to see me stay, and once Stasia leaves, there won't be a car here anyone could see either. I think we're safe for tonight." It was a heady feeling, but one he'd enjoy more if Royce wasn't acting oddly. "It really is up to you."

"Then stay."

"Okay." Shawn took Royce's outstretched hand and turned to Anastasia. "Guess you're heading home on your own. Do you need help getting the wine out to the car?"

"I'm good." Anastasia picked up her bag with her three bottles of wine and balanced it on her hip. "Have fun." She waved as she walked out the door.

Shawn shoved his hands in his pockets as he watched Royce lock the door and kept them there as he followed Royce to the back of the shop and up the stairs. This wasn't how he'd imagined tonight going, but he was determined to figure out what had Royce acting so off tonight. Royce hadn't given up on him despite his issues with Henry, and he'd be damned if he wouldn't do everything he could to return the favor.

This thing between them had become something he was willing to fight for.

16

ROYCE took a deep breath at the top of the stairs, trying to center himself before he opened the door to his apartment. He could feel Shawn standing behind him and hear the cats on the other side of the door, all anxious for him to open it, but he couldn't without taking a moment to figure out what he was doing. He wanted Shawn here, that part wasn't in question, but what he wanted to do and how far he was willing to take things was. He needed to figure it out, and fast.

Shawn shuffled and cleared his throat, drawing Royce out if his thoughts. "Everything all right?"

"Yeah. Just trying to decide if I want to let the cats run free or try to keep them up here. They're going to bolt as soon as I open the door." Puck and Kirra both hated tasting nights since Royce didn't let them in the shop when it was that crowded, and their reactions after were always interesting. Usually, they would go sniff everything downstairs to be sure it was all accounted for and then come back up so they could more effectively ignore him, but occasionally they did other things. A few times, they'd missed Royce more than the ability to go downstairs and had spent the rest of the night winding around his legs and climbing on him if he stopped for more than three seconds. Once, Puck had punished him by yowling all night, and another time he'd hidden for the entire next day.

Shawn bought the half truth. "Let 'em run," he said, seemingly unconcerned about the idea of two cats tearing past him down the stairs. "If they're down there, they won't be demanding attention from us."

That was a fair point, though part of Royce wanted them to stick around and provide distraction while he got his thoughts in order. "Okay," he said as he started to turn the doorknob. "You asked for it."

The cats shoved their way through the door as soon as Royce cracked it open. Kirra tumbled over Puck in her haste to get out and for a moment it looked like she was going to fall down the stairs. She found her feet on the third step down just as Puck barreled through the doorway, and they raced down to the shop, Kirra winning by a body length.

Shawn blinked at the cats as they disappeared into the shop. "They were impatient."

Royce laughed as he led the way into his living room. "They don't like to be in the shop when there are a lot of people there, but they hate to be told they can't go somewhere. Clearly, any place I'm trying to keep them out of is the best place ever, even if they've been there before."

"Oh, of course." Shawn followed Royce over to the couch. "Clearly, if you lock them out of a room, you must be using it for something so amazing that you want to keep it all for yourself."

"They'll be thrilled you understand their pain so well." Now if only Shawn would understand Royce's dilemma as well as he understood the cats. Unfortunately, getting Shawn to understand meant Royce had to explain it, and he wasn't sure he could properly articulate what he'd been feeling since their date last Saturday. He wasn't sure he wanted to bring it up yet.

"I'm sure they will." Shawn leaned back on the couch, angling his body toward Royce.

It would have been easy for Royce to press himself against Shawn's side, but instead he sat a few inches away, giving himself the room he needed to think without being obvious about it. "You want to watch a movie?" If he put on something he'd seen before, he could sit with Shawn and mull over what, if anything, he wanted to say.

Shawn didn't look thrilled with the movie idea. "I want to know why you've been acting off all night," he said, giving Royce a pointed look. "Was it because Stasia was here? I know she's… direct sometimes, but she means well. I can tell her to back off more if you want."

So much for time to think. "Stasia is fine," Royce said wearily. Tonight she'd helped emphasize the oddity of their arrangement in Royce's mind, especially when Shawn started flirting, but he liked her and was usually happy to see her, directness and all. "She's no worse than Clint, anyway."

"Oh." Shawn looked down at his lap and picked at his jeans. "So it was Saturday, then. I pushed too far."

"No. Yes." Royce rubbed his hand over his face as he tried to gather his thoughts. Saturday had been wonderful, except it had shown him what he was missing when they stayed in Portland on their dates. "Yes, Saturday, but not because you pushed too far."

"Then what?" Shawn didn't look up. "Was it bad?"

Royce wanted to take Shawn's hand and reassure him everything would be all right—a sign he was far more invested in this than he thought he could get in just a few months—but he needed distance if he was going to get his thoughts in order. "It was *not* bad," he said, trying to reassure Shawn with his voice alone. "It was good. Too good, maybe."

That got Shawn's attention, and he turned to look at Royce with a quizzical expression. "Too good? How can it be too good?"

"It made me want more." Now Royce was having trouble looking at Shawn, but he made himself meet Shawn's eyes as he struggled to find the right words. "I know I agreed to whatever you needed to keep Henry from finding out about us, and I meant that. But Saturday, we didn't have to worry, and everything felt different. I liked spending time with you and not worrying about your boss or who might see us or what was appropriate to do. I don't want to go back to hiding."

He held up his hand when Shawn opened his mouth. "Let me finish, please." He needed to get this all out before he was distracted by Shawn's answer. "Tonight just confused me. You've been flirting all night, even with all the other people here, and I don't know what to think about that. Was it because Anastasia was here and you could play it off as flirting with her if anyone asked, or because I was at work and couldn't really respond, or what? I don't know that I'm still willing to hide things, but if I am, we need clear boundaries."

Shawn waited a beat. "Can I answer now?" When Royce nodded, he took a deep breath and let it out slowly. "Okay. I don't know if I still want to buy Delicto."

That was not the answer Royce had been expecting. "You don't? Why not? What do you want to do?"

"I don't know. That's the problem. But I don't know that I can stay at Delicto, even just long enough to be able to buy it. Henry has been worse lately. He doesn't trust me with anything anymore, and I honestly don't know that I want to give him my money."

"Shit."

"Pretty much." Shawn laughed hollowly. "I've been trying to figure out what else I can do, but it's hard. Other than a vague notion that maybe someday I might do something with my art, owning Delicto has been my only real goal. I don't know what else to do."

"You'll figure it out," Royce said confidently. He had no doubt Shawn could find something and be amazing at whatever it was. He had the same sort of drive that had enabled Royce to make All

Corked Up so successful. He simply needed somewhere to direct his energy. "If I can help in any way...."

"You do help. A lot, actually. I never realized how miserable hiding things from Henry made me until it affected things between us." He paused and smiled wryly. "And Stasia beat me over the head with the fact that I wasn't acting like myself. She actually yelled at me for not calling her any mean nicknames."

"I've never heard you call her anything but Anastasia and Stasia." Royce wondered what else Shawn could have called her. There weren't many nicknames that sprung to mind. "What did she want to be called?"

"I don't think 'want' is the right word. I used to call her mean things like Spacey Stacy and Anesthesia just because I could."

"And now?"

"I've been too caught up in you and everything that's happening with Henry to think of any new nicknames. Besides, she's pounded enough sense into me lately that she probably deserves a break from the mean names."

"Probably?" From what Royce had seen, Anastasia deserved more than that, though he wasn't going to question the dynamics of her relationship with Shawn. It worked and gave Shawn the support he needed. That was all Royce really cared about.

"All right, definitely. But I might have to pull the nicknames back out if she keeps pushing art commissions on me."

"Art commissions?" Royce still hadn't seen any of Shawn's art. As far as he knew, Shawn didn't show it to many people. "How is she getting you art commissions?"

"Well, art *commission*. If I take it. It's one of her Navy buddies. Apparently, he saw the painting I gave her for her birthday last year and wanted to know if I would do something for him."

The hint of jealousy that had surged up at the idea of strangers being invited to see Shawn's work when he wasn't faded. "Are you going to?"

"Probably, this time, because Stasia's asking," Shawn said ruefully. "She suggested I could try to sell art to help if I quit Delicto, but I want to enjoy it, not have to do it."

"You probably don't want to sell it, then. Doing one for Stasia's friend is one thing, but I don't think you want to make a career out of it. You'd have to show too many people."

"Is that a hint? Am I supposed to show you?"

"I'd like to see it when you're comfortable showing me." Or right now, but Royce knew better than to push. "I guess it really depends on what we decide."

"Yeah." Shawn looked down at his hands.

Royce's stomach dropped. That wasn't a good sign. Had he pushed too far? Said too much? He didn't want Shawn out of his life, and if that meant they had to keep hiding, he would. "We don't have to stop. We can go to the vineyards or Eugene for every date, if you want."

"No." Shawn turned so he was sitting sideways on the couch and looked straight at Royce. He looked more serious and more uncertain than Royce had ever seen him. "That's not what I want."

A little bit of hope unfurled deep inside Royce. "Then what?"

"I'm done hiding too." Shawn glanced down, biting his lip, but looked up before Royce could respond. "I'm not going to drag you into Delicto and make out with you in front of Henry or anything, but I'm not going to refuse to be seen with you in public either. I love you, and I'm not going to hide that."

Royce opened his mouth, shut it again, and replayed Shawn's words in his head. "Oh." That was not where he'd imagined this conversation going. He'd had images of Shawn insisting they hide and threatening to break it off if Royce wouldn't, not agreeing and confessing his feelings. "Really?"

"Really." Shawn laughed and the sound brightened Royce's entire apartment. "I know it's harder for you to get away with Clint gone, but when he gets back, I thought maybe we could go to dinner at Portland Prime?"

"Isn't that the kind of restaurant Henry would go to?"

"Yes. But it's also a nice date-night restaurant, so I really don't care."

"Oh." Royce thought about that for a minute, imagined sitting there with Shawn, not caring who saw them or what anyone said, and thought this was probably what his mother meant when she said she was over the moon about something. The mere idea, coupled with Shawn's earlier confession, left Royce feeling so light and happy he was honestly surprised his body was still firmly on the couch. "Okay."

"It's a date." Shawn settled back on the couch, this time pressing the entire length of his body against Royce's. "Of course, so is this, so… how about that movie?"

Royce's entire right side was warm where Shawn was pressed against him, and his heart fluttered every time he thought about what Shawn had confessed. "In a minute." He put his fingers on the side of Shawn's jaw, turned his head so they were looking at each other, and kissed him gently.

Shawn kissed him back, but it stayed soft. Somehow, this, with their lips slowly moving together and their bodies pressed side by side on the couch, was more intimate than what they'd done in the car on Saturday, and more thrilling than the illicit kiss they'd stolen in the back room. When they broke apart, Royce could barely remember why he'd been worried tonight. This was right and natural, everything he'd imagined before giving up on the idea of love to run All Corked Up, and he couldn't believe the idea of giving up on it because of someone else had even crossed his mind.

"I love you," he whispered softly enough Shawn might not have heard him if not for the complete silence in the apartment. He hadn't planned on saying it yet, hadn't even been sure he felt it until he realized how panicked he was at the idea of Shawn calling things off, but there was no reason not to say it now.

Shawn's answering smile made it all worth it. "Oh," he said, though he was clearly teasing and not stunned like Royce had been. "Really?"

Royce laughed and shook his head. "Yes. Really. Is that so hard to believe?"

Shawn's answer was almost lost in the thunder of Puck and Kirra racing up the stairs, but Royce heard it anyway. "Not at all."

17

ROYCE'S good mood hadn't faded one bit by the time Clint came back a week and a half later. He was ringing up a customer when Clint walked in and leaned against the counter. He couldn't say anything until they were alone in the shop, but he brightened a little just knowing Clint was back and he and Shawn would be going to Portland Prime on Saturday.

By the time the customers left, Clint had clearly caught on, and he looked at Royce with a raised eyebrow. "Someone's in a good mood. Did you get laid while I was gone?"

"No." Royce tried to use a tone that would discourage Clint from probing further, but he knew going in it was a vain hope.

"Really? 'Cause you sure look a hell of a lot more satisfied than you were when I left." Clint leaned on the counter, using it to boost himself up so he was at eye level with Royce. "*Something* happened while I was gone. What?"

"Shawn and I had a few dates, that's all. Nothing you need to worry about." As much as Clint wanted to live vicariously through his relationship with Shawn, Royce wasn't ready to share what had happened after the tasting just yet. "How's your mother?"

"She's fine. She was up to her usual state of nagging me about my life last weekend. The past four days have been delightful." Clint rolled his eyes. "Now, stop deflecting. Something else happened. Share."

Royce's first instinct was to flat-out refuse, but that would be as good as admitting something had happened, and then Clint wouldn't let up until he got every not-so-sordid detail. "Why are you so sure?"

Clint dropped down to stand flat on the floor and looked at Royce incredulously. "I'm going to lose every bit of credibility I have by saying this, but you're fucking *glowing*. I could see your joy from the door, and as glad as I am to be home, I know it's not because you're happy to see me."

"Actually...." Royce chuckled at Clint's stunned look. It was always fun to be able to shock him. "I am happy to see you, but not like that. Shawn and I have been waiting for you to get back so we can go to Portland Prime without worrying about the shop."

Clint stepped away from the counter, radiating skepticism. "Is the shop really your biggest concern if you're going to Portland Prime? Shouldn't you be worried about his asshole of a boss finding out?"

"Shawn doesn't care." Royce still couldn't believe his good fortune. He didn't doubt Shawn at all, but it was almost too good to be true. Sometimes it felt more like a dream than reality. "He came to the last tasting, and we talked after and...." Royce sighed happily, lost in his memories of the night.

Clint's mouth dropped open. "You bastard. You told him how you feel, didn't you?" Royce's face burned, more than enough confirmation for Clint. "You haven't even gotten laid yet!"

Royce glared at him. Yes, he wanted to take things further with Shawn, but other than that night in the car, they just hadn't gone that way yet. He wasn't holding back or anything, and he didn't think Shawn was either. Not anymore. "It's not about the sex, Clint."

"Yeah, yeah." Clint waved his hand dismissively. "It's all connection and feelings and happy fluffy bunnies."

"I think the cats would eat any fluffy bunnies I brought home."

"I don't know, man, bunnies can be vicious."

Royce flipped him off, ending the conversation before he had to explain to Clint again how companionship could be worth more than sex. He'd figure that out eventually. "Did you come here to work or just give me a hard time?"

Clint shrugged out of his jacket and hung it on the hook behind the counter. "I guess 'both' isn't a valid answer? If I have to pick, I'll pick work, but I'm not sure I can get through a whole shift without giving you a hard time. It *has* been almost three weeks."

Royce shot Clint an exasperated look. "Just get to work. I'm going to take care of some things in the back."

"Aye-aye." Clint saluted lazily as he moved to take Royce's place behind the counter.

Royce ignored it but paused before heading to his office. "You sure everything is okay with your mother?"

"I wouldn't have come back if it wasn't," Clint said in a tone that strongly implied Royce was an idiot for asking. "Now go. Get your shit done so I can interrogate you about Shawn guilt-free."

Royce waved him off as he headed upstairs. "I will find a way to make you feel guilty."

The door closed on Clint's reply.

ROYCE had made it about halfway through the paperwork he'd been putting off when his phone buzzed. He glanced at the number, saw it was Clint, and started saving the file he was working on as he picked up the phone. "Yeah?"

"Your boy's here."

"He's not—"

"Don't even try to tell me he isn't yours. You have *feelings*."

Royce gently banged his head on the back of his chair a few times and let himself hope for just a moment that Clint hadn't said that in front of Shawn. "I was going to say he's not a boy."

"And how would you know that? I thought you hadn't gotten in each other's pants yet."

Royce scrambled for the door. He did *not* need Shawn to know he'd told Clint that. "Stop talking. Seriously. I'm coming down. Don't say another word until I get there." He ended the call so Clint wouldn't be tempted to respond and scurried the rest of the way down the stairs, the cats on his heels. They darted out in front of him when they reached the shop, Kirra heading straight to Clint to demand attention, and Puck sauntering up to Shawn in a way that suggested Shawn should be grateful for the opportunity to notice him.

Clint scooped Kirra up and laughed as she wriggled around, trying to get settled in his arms. "Did you miss me, girl? Hmm? Did Royce not give you enough attention?"

"I gave her plenty of attention," Royce said dryly. "You just spoil her."

"That's because she likes it," he said, leaning back so she wouldn't fall off as she tried to climb up on his shoulder while butting her head against him with every step and purring loudly.

"Of course she likes it. You let her get away with everything." Royce looped his arms around Shawn's neck and pulled him in for a swift kiss. "Hi."

Shawn pulled Royce in closer, put his hands on Royce's hips, and kissed him like Clint wasn't there. "Hey."

"Oh God," Clint said as he carefully pried Kirra's claws out of his shirt and set her down as he crouched to pay attention to Puck. "You were serious. He really doesn't care who sees him now."

"I never cared if you saw, anyway," Shawn said as he pulled Royce in for another kiss. Royce was certain this one was to make a point with Clint, but he wasn't going to object if it meant Shawn kissed him like that.

Clint held his hands up in surrender but immediately started petting Puck again when he meowed loudly. "No issue here. Just don't be all sappy at work, okay? I get enough listening to Jess wax poetic about her latest guy."

Royce frowned. He hadn't even known Jess had a latest guy, though to be fair she seemed to cycle through them quickly. "She hasn't said anything to me."

"Of course not." Clint stood, ignoring the cats' protests. "You're her boss. I'm her coworker. That means you only hear about the big, important things, but I get to hear all about Jess's boyfriends, Brandy's kids, and Lisa's travel plans."

"Lucky you." Shawn looked almost wistful, and it made Royce wonder just how bad things had gotten at Delicto. He knew Henry had been causing problems, but he hadn't known Shawn's coworkers were giving him trouble too.

Clint shrugged thoughtfully. "Well, it does sometimes give me good blackmail material."

That was exactly the right thing to say. Shawn laughed, the worry gone from his face. "Does Royce have a lot of blackmail material on you?"

"He has the authorized signature on the checking account our paychecks come from," Clint grumbled. "It's an amazingly effective way to get what he wants."

"And right now that's for you to work late Saturday so Shawn and I can go to Portland Prime."

"You sure that's what you want?" Clint looked straight at Shawn. "It's about damn time the two of you got your heads out of your asses and did something about this thing you have going on, but if your boss is as big an asshole as Royce says he is, then—"

"My boss can go screw himself."

Clint looked just as flummoxed as Royce felt. He knew Shawn was pissed at Henry and ready to be done with hiding, but he hadn't expected that reaction. Shawn was usually more levelheaded, and the difference left Royce floundering for something to say.

Clint found his composure before Royce and whistled. "Damn. You are annoyed. What are you going to do if he goes through with his threats?"

"Quit. Find something else to do or a different place to buy." Shawn worked his mouth into a very small but very kissable smile. "I haven't decided yet. I have the money I was saving for a down payment, though, so I don't need something lined up right away."

Royce bumped his shoulder against Shawn's. "I'm sure you'll find something fast. You have experience."

Shawn didn't look as confident as Royce hoped. "Depends on how things end with Henry. I'll be fine if he gives me a reference. If he doesn't... I'll figure something else out."

Clint snorted, sounding half annoyed and half amused. "If he refuses to give you references, invest here. Royce won't need your references, and he could use a kick in the ass to get the restaurant part started."

"I do not!" Okay, Royce might have been neglecting the planning a little as things heated up with Shawn, but it wasn't like he was on a specific schedule. "Besides, aren't *you* going to invest in it?"

"If you need me to." Clint shrugged, looking awfully unconcerned for someone who had put his own investments on hold to contribute to the very thing he was suggesting he give up. "My interest is in helping you and making sure this place sticks around, not actually investing in a restaurant. I'll find another house to flip instead. No problem."

"We don't even know what Henry is going to do yet," Shawn said in an amused tone. "He might not even see us before I have enough money to buy Delicto. I said I was done hiding, not that I was going to shove my decision in his face."

"Riiiight." Skepticism dripped from Clint's tone. "Because the geriatric crowd never frequents Portland Prime or any of the other 'date night' restaurants in town."

"I know it's a possibility," Shawn said slowly. "I just don't want to get ahead of myself, all right? I'll deal with whatever happens when it happens."

"I don't think discussing ideas is getting ahead of ourselves." Royce took a deep breath, trying to calm down a little. "We don't have to decide anything right now. *You* don't have to decide anything, I mean. It's all your decision. I'm happy to help if you want, but you're right. We don't know what Henry will do even if he does find out." Royce couldn't let himself think about the possibility of Shawn owning All Corked Up with him until they did. It was an exhilarating idea, but Royce didn't know if he wanted to kiss or kick Clint for suggesting it. If it worked, it would be a dream come true, but if things went sour between him and Shawn—a possibility he shuddered to contemplate—it would be an absolute nightmare.

Clint backed away, his hands in the air. "Just throwin' the idea out there. I only haven't been looking for a new house to flip because I thought you'd need me to invest. If you don't, it's no skin off my back."

Shawn looked skeptical, but he nodded. "We'll see." His dubious expression morphed into something entirely different as he turned to Royce. "Since Clint's back, you want to leave the cats to get reacquainted with him and you and I can pick up where we left off the other night?"

Twice now, they'd been upstairs making out, getting hot and heavy and in Royce's mind leading to more only to be interrupted by a chirping kitten squeezing between them and demanding attention. Royce thought they should have tossed her in the office or locked her downstairs, but Shawn, new to the manipulative ways of cats, had fallen for Kirra's entirely fake, wide-eyed, pitiful look and started petting her before Royce could say anything. That had naturally led to Puck joining them on the couch as well. Though Royce meant it when he said there was more to a relationship than sex, he was *very* tempted by the idea of having a few cat-free hours.

"That sounds wonderful." He scooped Kirra from the wine crates she'd climbed on and handed her to Clint. "We'll be back later."

"Take your time!" Clint called, laughing as Royce took Shawn's hand and practically pulled him to the stairs. "Don't do anything I wouldn't do!"

Royce pulled the door shut before Clint could say anything else or either cat could make a break for the stairs. "That doesn't eliminate much."

Shawn's face lit up like it was Christmas morning. "I don't have a problem with that."

18

SHAWN tapped the fingers of his free hand nervously against his leg as he and Royce walked into Portland Prime Steakhouse. He tried to keep his other hand—the one holding Royce's—still, but he must have given something away, because Royce stopped just before the door and pulled Shawn off to the side. "You okay?"

"Yeah." There were butterflies doing loop-de-loops in his stomach, his heart was trying to beat the rhythm of a fast dance in his chest, and he doubted he could stop fidgeting if his life depended on it, but he wasn't going to let any of that stop him. He wanted this, wanted to be here with Royce, no matter who saw them. Part of him hoped he'd run into Henry or one of his cronies just to get the inevitable confrontation over with, though the rest of him wanted a nice date in Portland where they didn't have to worry. They deserved that much.

Royce looked at him carefully, his concern evident on his face. "You sure?"

Yes." Shawn tugged Royce in for a swift kiss. There were people walking through the parking lot, and anyone looking out the window would be able to see them, but Shawn pushed those thoughts out of his mind and focused on Royce. He had planned to pull back after a quick brush of their lips, but he could feel Royce's surprise and it made him bold. He deepened the kiss, slid his tongue into Royce's mouth, and used his free hand to pull Royce closer and press their bodies together.

Royce gasped, then returned the kiss and the embrace. He pressed so close to Shawn it bordered on indecent, and if anyone had seen the way their tongues moved between their mouths, it would've been far beyond that.

Desire burned through Shawn, calming the butterflies, stilling his twitching fingers, and making his heart race for an entirely different reason. It was torture to pull back, but if he didn't, he wasn't sure he'd be able to stop himself later. Newfound confidence aside, the parking lot wasn't an appropriate place for where his mind was going.

Royce made a soft noise that did more to excite Shawn's libido than to calm it, then laughed shakily. "Okay. You're *really* not worried about who sees, huh?"

"I'm worried." It was easier to admit now. The kiss had given him focus. "I don't want anything to mess tonight up, though, including worrying so much I mess it up, so I'm trying not to think about it." Shawn squeezed Royce's hand. "I have better things to think about."

Royce leaned over and kissed Shawn's cheek. "I love you."

"I hope so," Shawn said with a smile. "I *am* putting my career in jeopardy for this."

"You're getting yourself out of a crappy career situation *because* of this," Royce said with so much conviction Shawn had no choice but to believe him.

"Or that." Shawn liked Royce's take on the idea better, though he wasn't convinced owning Delicto would be a bad situation once Henry was out of the picture. There was the potential for problems with current employees, of course. Shawn didn't have as many friends among them as he had before Henry stopped trusting him, but he still thought he could have made it work. The situation now was a crappy career situation, though, and Royce's idea made that easier to remember.

Royce pulled his phone from his pocket just long enough to glance at it. "We should let them know we're here. Do you want to wait here while I go in or...?"

"I'll come." It was a nice night in late April, not too cold or hot and not raining, but Shawn was ready to go in. If it was crowded and a long wait, they might come back out, but they had reservations, so Shawn doubted it would be an issue. "We can get a drink if there's a long wait."

"Or we could come back out here," Royce suggested with an impish wink that made Shawn's heart flutter. He wasn't sure how he was supposed to make it through dinner if Royce kept saying things like that. At least once they were inside, they would have a table between them and other people around to encourage Shawn to keep his hands to himself. They hadn't gotten past kissing and heavy petting yet, but damn if Shawn didn't want to do more of it.

"We'll see," he said, taking Royce's hand again and heading toward the door. The nervous feeling he'd fought off while kissing Royce returned, but he paid no attention to it. He figured it was just nerves again until they walked through the door and almost ran into a group of older men on their way out.

"Sorry," Shawn instinctively apologized. It was one of those situations where no one was clearly at fault, and Shawn had always been taught it was better to apologize than come across as rude.

The men they ran into either hadn't had the same lesson or else they felt they were entitled to the right of way. They grumbled and scowled, ignoring Shawn's apology as he tried to figure out the best way to get out of their path. He was about to step back outside when one of the men in the back pushed his way forward, stopping Shawn cold.

The very first time Shawn wasn't afraid of running into Henry while out with Royce on a real date, that was exactly what they did.

"Shawn," Henry said in the annoyed tone that had become his norm while talking to Shawn over the past few months. "What are you…. Oh." He curled his lip up in disgust as he looked down at Shawn and Royce's joined hands. "Is this the… person you were out with before?"

"It's a pleasure to meet you." Royce managed to make the lie sound natural as he extended his hand to Henry. "Shawn's told me a lot about you."

"I'm sure he has." Henry looked Royce over but didn't take his offered hand, and soon returned his gaze to Shawn. "I thought we agreed you weren't going to date men. You know I can't sell you Delicto if you insist on giving in to this depravity. I thought you were doing so well. I've seen you with that girl again."

"You insisted," Shawn clarified. "I wasn't given a choice."

"It shouldn't be a choice," one of the other men said. Shawn vaguely recognized him as someone who came into Delicto occasionally, but didn't know his name. "Henry always used to say such good things about you, Shawn. It's sad to see you've fallen in with the wrong crowd."

"The wrong crowd is people who insist they have the right to decide who I'm allowed to love, not the people who love me." Shawn looked Henry straight in the eyes. "I love Royce and he loves me. That isn't going to change."

Henry looked between Royce and Shawn, his expression growing more confused when Royce stepped closer and nodded. "But the girl!" he exclaimed, clearly thinking he'd caught on to something Royce didn't know about. "I've seen you with her a lot lately. What about her?"

"Anastasia? I've met her. She's Shawn's best friend," Royce scoffed. "Nothing more."

Shawn was sure he would never love Royce more than he did right then. "She's been around more because she's in the Navy and she just got done with a long cruise. Not that it's any of your concern."

"There's something between the two of you. Don't deny it." Henry put his hand on Shawn's arm. It was probably supposed to be comforting, but all it did was make Shawn itch to get away. "You're sick, Shawn, but this girl could help you get better. You don't have to give in to these urges."

Shawn bit back a laugh. He loved Anastasia, but their ill-fated relationship in college had been more than enough to convince him it was a platonic love. "I'm not sick, Henry. I'm gay."

Henry tightened his grip on Shawn's arm. "That is sick, Shawn, you just don't realize it. Let me help you. If not this girl, then another. You don't have to listen to this *man*." He shot Royce a look so dirty Shawn wanted to take a shower.

He twisted his arm free and glowered at Henry. "This *man* is the person I love."

"You know I can't sell you Delicto if you continue to act like this, Shawn." Henry looked genuinely sad at the prospect, and the men behind him murmured and shook their heads. "I have to think of the restaurant. Of the other employees. The customers just wouldn't stand for it."

Shawn suspected many of the customers would stand with him rather than Henry if they knew, but he wasn't going to change Henry's mind. He knew that. "Then don't sell it to me."

Royce tightened his grip on Shawn's hand, but that was the only outward sign of surprise he gave. Henry, on the other hand, looked absolutely flabbergasted, and the men behind him weren't much better. The gaggle of them standing in the entrance to Portland Prime with their eyes wide and their jaws dropped would have been a hilarious sight if Shawn hadn't wanted to deck each and every one of them.

The restaurant host took advantage of the pause and diffidently stepped up to the group. "Is there a problem, gentlemen?"

Shawn forced a smile he no longer felt. "No. Everything is fine. We just didn't expect to run into each other here."

"In that case, I have to ask you to step away from the entrance, please. If you're waiting for a table, you're welcome to wait inside. Otherwise, I hope you enjoyed your meal and we look forward to seeing you again soon."

"Of course." Royce inclined his head gracefully. "I believe these men were leaving, and we're coming in." He stepped neatly to the side, pulling Shawn with him. Most of Henry's cronies obediently filed out, grumbling under their breaths as they passed. Shawn couldn't pick out more than a few words, but he imagined they were going on about the audacity of youth these days, and the decline of morals in society.

Henry, however, stayed. He stepped to the side with Shawn and Royce and put his hand on Shawn's elbow again. "You don't mean that."

"Yes, I do." Shawn pulled his elbow free from Henry and let go of Royce's hand. He appreciated the support, but he needed to say this on his own. He needed Henry to know he was serious, Royce to see how committed he was, and to show himself he could really go through with this. "Find someone else to sell Delicto to, Henry."

"You can't just back out," Henry blustered, drawing himself up to his full height and poking Shawn in the chest. "We had an agreement."

"An *informal* agreement." Shawn pushed Henry's finger away. "You agreed to sell Delicto to me when I had the money. *You* changed the agreement when you tried to make that contingent on how I live my life. You get to tell me what I can and can't do when I'm at work, but you have no right to tell me who I can date."

"I have the right to worry about the image of my company."

"And if I were off doing drugs or hurting people, you'd have a point!" The background murmur in the restaurant faded, and Shawn winced. He hadn't meant to say that quite so loudly. "I'm going on a *date*, Henry. Royce is a respected business owner. There is *nothing* I have done with Royce that would negatively affect the image of Delicto." Nothing they'd been caught doing, anyway, and even in the car at the vineyard and in the parking lot just now, they hadn't done anything horrible. It might have scandalized a few sensitive people—the same ones Henry was worried about offending—but he doubted most people would be too bothered.

Henry huffed. "Dating *him* is negatively affecting the image of Delicto. You're flaunting your disease, Shawn, and I can't have that. Let me help you find a nice girl to settle down with. You'll be happier."

This time, Shawn did laugh. He hadn't dated any women after Anastasia, but there had been a few before her, and none had been what he really wanted. "No, I won't. Stop trying, Henry. You don't get any say in who I date." He leaned in close as Henry opened his mouth to protest. "If you keep insisting you do, you can find a new manager too. I'm not going to work for you if you keep treating me like this."

"You're—"

"Don't say it." Shawn looked around, taking in the way the host was watching them warily and the attention they'd attracted from all the other patrons in the restaurant, and made a decision. "Consider this my notice, Henry. I'll work the current schedule, but find someone else to take over before you make the new one. I'm done."

As Henry sputtered, Shawn stepped around him and motioned for Royce to follow. "I'm sorry for the disturbance," he said to the host. "We'll be leaving now. You can cancel our reservation. It's under Wilkinson." He stepped outside then, glancing at the men waiting for Henry just to the left of the door. One of them tried to stop him, but Shawn kept walking. These assholes had ruined his date before it had really started. He was through dealing with them.

Henry wasn't as easy to get rid of. He followed Shawn outside, pushed past him, and then stood blocking his path. In other circumstances, Shawn might have been shocked at how fast he'd moved, but tonight he was just annoyed. "Don't," he said before Henry could catch his breath enough to talk. "I meant what I said. You can't expect me to stick around the way you've been treating me, so save your breath. You're not going to change my mind. Stop trying."

"You're going to regret this someday."

Shawn smiled as he took in Henry's anger and Royce's steady presence at his side. He thought about how Royce had been willing to do whatever it took to be with him while Henry had made unreasonable demands for him to stay on his chosen career path. He thought about how happy he was with Royce and how miserable he'd been every day at work, and he knew without a doubt that he'd made the right decision. "No, I won't."

He took Royce's hand and stepped around Henry again. "Have a good night, Henry." This time, Henry didn't follow.

Shawn made it around the corner before he was hit with a sudden wave of giddiness and relief. He stopped, unable to hold back giggles, and leaned into Royce's shoulder. "Fuck, that felt good."

"Looked good too," Royce said, his voice a low growl in Shawn's ear. "I never thought I'd be thrilled to leave a restaurant without eating, but I don't think I could have made it through dinner without jumping you right there."

Shawn's breath hitched as his giddiness was replaced by desire. "My place is closer." He hadn't invited Royce over yet because he hadn't wanted his neighbors to see anything that might get back to Henry, but he saw no reason to worry about that now.

"Let's go, then. We need to celebrate you telling off your homophobic asshole of a boss, and we can't do that properly here."

He stepped back and looked at Shawn with a wicked gleam in his eyes. "I have plans that aren't appropriate in public."

Shawn swallowed hard, nodded when he couldn't find his voice, and started walking at a pace just shy of a run. How the fuck was he supposed to make it back to his apartment with Royce looking at him like that?

19

THEY made it five blocks before Royce pulled Shawn into an alley, pushed him against the brick wall, and paused for a second to look at him. Shawn's hair was disheveled, windblown, and the flush in his face was likely from exertion, not anger, but damn if Royce didn't find him as attractive now as he had back at Portland Prime when he was finally—finally!—standing up to Henry. Just the memory of Shawn standing there, radiating righteous anger was enough to make Royce surge forward. He pressed the entire length of their bodies together as he pinned Shawn to the wall and kissed him so deeply Shawn couldn't possibly mistake his intent.

Shawn moaned into the kiss and thrust his hips forward, pressing his erection into Royce's hip. He was as ready as Royce was, his cock's size apparent through the layers of clothing separating them. Royce wanted nothing more than to unzip Shawn's pants and wrap his lips around it, but they were still in public. They didn't have to worry about Henry anymore, but that didn't mean they could throw their reputations to the wind.

Instead, Royce rocked his hips forward, grinding his cock against Shawn's, and pushed his tongue into Shawn's mouth. Shawn parted his lips, letting Royce's tongue move freely, and grabbed Royce's hips, holding them loosely as they moved together. The noises Shawn made as they rutted connected straight to Royce's groin with a thread that pulled him insistently toward release, and the sounds he was making had more place in a porno than his mouth.

With great effort, Royce pulled back from the kiss. He braced his hands on Shawn's shoulders as he tried to focus, a difficult task with Shawn still pressing his cock into his hip. "How far to your apartment?" He'd only intended to kiss Shawn here, to let Shawn know how turned on he was by the way he'd stood up to Henry, but he wasn't sure he could stop now.

"Too far." Shawn leaned in for another kiss. As he distracted Royce with his tongue, he flipped them around and trapped Royce against the wall with his larger frame. "We need to finish this first."

The low timbre of Shawn's voice, combined with the way he was pressing Royce to the rough brick wall, was almost enough to make Royce come right then. He shivered and reached for another kiss, stretching his neck out so far it felt like he was baring his throat. Shawn took advantage, nibbling on the sensitive skin where Royce's neck met his shoulder, and it was again almost his undoing. "Shawn," he whispered, beyond protesting now.

"You can't shove me up against the wall in an alley and think we can *keep walking*." Shawn rolled his hips forward, and Royce gasped as their cocks touched. "You want this."

Royce did. *God,* he did, and the reasons they shouldn't seemed so insignificant now. With Shawn looking at him through blown pupils and pressing their groins together, it was hard to remember anything beyond the cold press of brick on his back and the fiery pressure of Shawn at his front. "We shouldn't," he managed, but it was a token protest and it was obvious Shawn knew it.

"Yeah."

Royce wrapped his arms around Shawn's shoulders for extra leverage and pulled him in for a searing kiss. Shawn slid his hands under Royce's ass, lifted him, and used the wall to hold him up as

Royce folded his legs around Shawn's waist. Without breaking the kiss, Royce started moving up and down, ignoring the bricks scraping against his back and focusing on the way Shawn rocked his hips forward to meet Royce's downward thrusts.

It took them a few tries to find the right rhythm, but once they did, it was the hottest thing Royce had ever done. Shawn had just enough of a height advantage to make holding Royce up advantageous. Every thrust sent shivers up his spine, every scrape of brick on his back brought him closer to climax. He tried to hold on, tried to make this last, but the memories of Shawn being a badass combined with the sensations overwhelming his brain were too much.

He muffled his scream in Shawn's shoulder as he came and slid down to stand on unsteady feet as Shawn shuddered against him. "Fuck," he whispered, letting his head fall back against the wall, trying to catch his breath.

"Yeah." Shawn leaned against him, pinning him to the wall much like he had earlier, only this time, there was nothing sexual to it. Shawn's presence in front of Royce was comforting now, shielding him from anyone who might walk by and glance into the alley.

It couldn't shield him forever, though. They had to leave, and soon, before they attracted attention. "We should shower," Royce said, making a face at the stickiness in his pants. The idea of walking to Shawn's apartment like this was unappealing, but not as unappealing as waiting in the alley and letting it dry. The sooner they got to Shawn's, the sooner Royce could see what Shawn was hiding under his clothes. After what he'd felt earlier, that was competing with getting clean for top priority in Royce's mind.

THE moment Royce was safely in Shawn's apartment, he shoved his pants and boxers down his legs and kicked them off, losing his shoes in the process. It felt so much better to have them off, though some of the half-dried jizz stayed on his skin as he removed his clothes. He wiped at it ineffectively and made a face as some of the sticky substance transferred to his hand. "Yeah. Not doing that again."

"I hope you mean the part where it was in an alley and not the rest," Shawn said as he pushed his pants down to his ankles.

"More the part where we were fully clothed and then walked eight blocks." Royce smiled wryly. "But yes, the alley part too." It had been incredibly hot, but at least bordered on illegal, and it wasn't something he wanted to make a habit of even if they hadn't broken any laws. He had a reputation to think about and employees to consider. Clint and the girls would never forgive him if he destroyed everything he'd built with All Corked Up for something as stupid as not being able to keep his hands out of Shawn's pants in public.

"Fair enough," Shawn conceded as he toed off his shoes and stepped out of the clothing pooled around his ankles. "The walking back in jizz-covered clothes wasn't that great."

"The rest of it was, though." Now that he wasn't walking in dirty underwear, Royce found it easier to remember the spectacular parts, like the way Shawn had stepped up and taken control. It wasn't something Royce was going to let him get away with all the time, but damn if it hadn't been fantastically hot, especially after the way Shawn had stood his ground in the restaurant.

"It was." Shawn advanced toward Royce with a predatory gleam in his eyes. He looked a little ridiculous with his cock bobbing just under the hem of his shirt and his long legs and knobby knees uncovered, but his stride was pure confidence.

Royce put his hand on Shawn's chest when he was close enough and stopped him. "Uh-uh. Shower."

Shawn pulled Royce's hand away, held his wrist loosely between thumb and finger, and leaned in for a kiss. "Laundry, *then* shower. Give me your shirt."

The idea of clean clothes waiting for him later was too tempting to resist. Royce pulled his shirt over his head and handed it to Shawn. "Where's the shower?" He figured he could get the water running while Shawn started the wash, and they'd have a fairly decent chance of getting the sweat and come off before they got dirty again.

"Off the bedroom at the end of the hall." Shawn scooped their pants and underwear from the floor. "I'll be there in a minute."

Royce didn't intend to explore Shawn's apartment before they showered, but as he walked down the hall, he glanced through the open door of what he thought was a spare bedroom and saw an art studio instead. Curious, he went inside and stood in the middle of the room, looking at dozens of drawings and paintings hung on and propped against the wall.

He recognized some of the subjects as characters from various television shows and movies, but it was the other pieces that really caught his eye. Gorgeous, impossible landscapes surrounded fantastic creatures in some of the more elaborate pieces. In one, a griffin soared over a crystal lake, squawking at the giant serpent looking out of the rippling water. In another, a black unicorn fiercely defended a newborn phoenix as it rose from the ashes and the burnt-out trees around them miraculously grew new blooms. In a third, two winged men washed each other under a waterfall in a magical-looking grotto.

There were simpler pictures too, focusing just on the creatures rather than incorporating elaborate backgrounds, but no less amazing because of it. A brownie chugged a jug of milk in one. A winged kitten that looked suspiciously like Kirra pounced on a ball of yarn in another. A drunk pixie tumbled out of a beer stein in a third.

Royce walked around the room slowly, looking at everything and growing more impressed with Shawn's talent with each one he passed. On the desk, Royce found two unfinished pieces, one half buried beneath the other. The top one was a sketch of a dragon curled around something. The giant lizard was drawn in great detail, clearly ready to be gone over with whatever medium Shawn used for the final piece, but the thing it was curled around was light circles and squares that didn't make anything Royce could decipher.

The second piece was a beach with vague shapes drawn near the water. They were all roughly the same size, but some looked like they'd eventually transform into animals, while others were upright, like people, and one was halfway between the two. Royce slid the paper out from under the dragon picture to see if the rest of the piece held more clues to what the shapes would eventually be, but the only thing on the other side of the picture was a rock jutting out of the water.

"They're selkies," Shawn said from the doorway, startling Royce enough that he stepped back from the desk. "It's the piece Stasia's friend commissioned."

"Oh." Royce clasped his hands behind his back so he wouldn't be tempted to touch again and tried to fight down the feeling of having done something horrible. "Sorry. I shouldn't have come in here. I was going to have the shower all ready."

"It doesn't take long to start a shower," Shawn said wryly. "And it's fine. If I cared about you wandering through my apartment, I wouldn't have sent you ahead."

That was a valid point, but it didn't change the fact that Royce had gone into the studio uninvited. "Still. I shouldn't have snooped."

"I'd hardly call looking at pieces that are set out where anyone can see snooping. If you dug through the drawers looking for more, *that* would be snooping. Pulling the selkies out from under the dragon doesn't count." Shawn bumped his shoulder against Royce's. "Stop worrying. I was going to show you later anyway."

Royce couldn't decide if it was weirder that Shawn was so calm or that they were having this conversation buck naked. "You were?"

"You did ask to see it."

"Well, yeah, but…." Royce tried to think of the best way to articulate his thoughts. Shawn was secretive about his art, and Royce hadn't expected to see it yet. He couldn't decide if he was pleased Shawn had decided to show him or disappointed he'd missed Shawn's introduction to it.

Shawn laughed, though Royce couldn't tell if it was at Royce's conundrum or the absurdity of the situation. "I was going to show you the room and tell you to look all you wanted," he said with a self-deprecating shrug. "I don't really like to watch when other people look at my stuff. I'm always convinced they'll hate it."

Royce gaped at him. "How could people possibly hate these? They're *fantastic*!"

"I think as my boyfriend you're required to say that."

"I think as your boyfriend, I'm required to be honest with you." Royce looked around again and tried to pick a favorite, but he couldn't. He liked each piece more than the last and could have gushed easily about any of them. "Seriously, Shawn, this stuff is phenomenal. I know you don't want to sell it, but Stasia is right. It's good enough to sell."

Shawn shrugged and looked down, clearly not convinced. "They're not as good as the stuff you see in galleries."

"Maybe not." Royce could have argued the point, but it wasn't worth it tonight. "But I'd rather have any of these on my wall than most of the stuff galleries charge thousands for. It's not for everyone because it's fantasy and I know there are people who don't like the genre, but that doesn't mean it isn't amazing work."

Shawn shuffled his feet. "I guess."

The last thing Royce wanted was for Shawn to be uncomfortable. That didn't bode well for the rest of the evening or for him getting to see more of Shawn's work. "Well, I like them," he said firmly as he headed toward the door. "Can I tell you that?"

"I suppose." Shawn still looked a little embarrassed, but he smiled as he followed Royce out into the hallway. "Did you see the kitten with wings? I based her on Kirra, though I think I might have gotten some of the coloring wrong. I was working from memory and—"

"It looked just like her, right down to the white splotch on her nose. That *is* Kirra." Royce paused and watched Shawn light up. "Well, except for the wings, of course. And Kirra would manage to tangle herself in a ball of yarn, not pounce on it that neatly."

Shawn threw back his head and laughed. "She would, wouldn't she? I know you're not supposed to give cats yarn because it can hurt them if they eat it, but she *definitely* shouldn't have any. She'd tie herself up and fall down the stairs!"

She would, too. Despite being about six months old now, Kirra still hadn't found her sense of balance. She loved to walk on the arms and back of Royce's couch, but she managed to fall off half the time, and Royce couldn't count the number of times she'd slowly slid off his lap. It was as if she didn't recognize the sensation of falling until it was too late to stop herself and she ended up on the floor, chirping indignantly as Royce was torn between amusement and concern.

"I don't even want to think about what trouble that cat would get into if I gave her yarn."

Shawn looked over his shoulder at Royce as he started the shower. "Because it's too horrifying to contemplate or because you have much better things to think about tonight?"

Royce's cock stirred at the sight of Shawn reached over, adjusting the shower temperature as water splashed onto him. "Both," he said, putting his hands on Shawn's hips. "But mostly the second."

"Good." Shawn put his hands over Royce's and kept them in place as he led Royce into the shower stall. "I seem to recall promising a little fun in the shower."

"More than a *little*, I think." Royce pushed forward until he had Shawn pressed against the shower wall and leaned against his back. His cock brushed against the crack of Shawn's ass as he stretched up onto his toes and kissed Shawn's neck just below his ear. "If I remember right, you promised to make this the best shower I've ever taken." He'd said it jokingly as they walked back to Shawn's apartment, but now that he had Shawn naked and wet in front of him, Royce saw no reason not to take Shawn at his word.

Shawn turned around so his back was against the shower wall and pulled Royce in closer. "I did, didn't I?" He slid his hands down to Royce's ass and squeezed. "I should do that, then."

Royce slid his hand between them and wrapped it around Shawn's cock. The idea of letting Shawn take over and fulfill his promise was a nice one, but after letting Shawn take control in the alley, Royce wanted his turn. "Or you could let me give *you* the best shower you've ever taken."

Shawn's eyes widened a fraction, but he looked pleased as he met Royce's gaze. "You think you can?"

That was a challenge if Royce had ever heard one, but he was up for it. Naked, Shawn was as gorgeous as Royce had imagined in the alley, with a sprinkling of hair on his chest and smooth abs. Shawn's cock was everything Royce had imagined too, and he squeezed it gently and slid his hand down to rub his thumb over the tip. "Absolutely."

Shawn shivered as Royce fondled his balls. "Then stop teasing."

"Not teasing." Royce fully intended to turn Shawn around and pound him into the shower wall, but first he was going to take Shawn apart bit by bit and appreciate every moment of it. "I'm just getting warmed up."

20

SHAWN groaned, let his head fall back against the tiles, and looked at Royce through his eyelashes. Water drops glistened on Royce's tanned skin, making him almost glow in the muted light, and turned into rivulets that cascaded over his shoulders and down his chest as he stepped under the shower spray. Shawn watched one drop roll all the way down to the curls of dark hair at Royce's groin, admiring the firm roundness of Royce's pecs and the softer curves of his stomach. Royce had muscles from lifting cases of wine, but he wasn't a fitness nut, and Shawn found the lack of a six-pack amazingly attractive

His dick twitched as he watched Royce stand under the water. He curled one hand around it since Royce had let go and slowly pumped up and down, bringing it into full hardness. "Warm up faster."

Royce watched with an appreciative look on his face. "Don't come. You don't want to spoil the fun."

"Then *do something*." Shawn was all for taking things slowly, but this was a glacial pace. Unless Royce considered standing in front of Shawn with water running over him foreplay—and an argument could be made in favor of that—Shawn was going to do all the work and be done before Royce started.

"What do you want me to do?" Royce wrapped his hand around his cock and slowly stroked it as Shawn watched. "Would you like me to spin you around, finger you open, and pound you into the wall? Or do you want me to drop down to my knees and suck you so hard you can't stand? Maybe I should push you down to your knees and have you suck me. Or should I kiss you and finger you until we're both so hard we can't stand it and you come without me even touching your cock?"

The list of ideas was intoxicating. Shawn stilled his hand as he imagined each of them in vivid detail. Each was more appealing than the last, and there was only one he was able to easily eliminate from the list of possibilities. "Not the first, but any of the others. I like sucking. And fingering. And kissing."

"I can do that." Royce stepped forward, put his hand on Shawn's chest, and leaned up to kiss him. As their tongues tangled, Royce slid his hand down to cover Shawn's. He pumped a few times, drawing Shawn right up to the brink, and then pulled both their hands away from Shawn's cock. "Not touching your cock, remember?"

"Fuck that," Shawn growled, suddenly sure what he wanted. "Touch. Suck. *Please*."

Royce put his hands on Shawn's hips. "You or me?"

"Both." Shawn dropped to his knees and pulled Royce with him. "Gonna suck you off while you do the same for me."

Royce made an appreciative noise as he gracefully folded to his knees. "Yes," he whispered as he pushed Shawn back to lie on the shower floor with his head away from the spray.

The water hit Shawn right on his groin. He bent his knees, slid down so it hit his chest instead, and let his legs fall open in a blatant invitation Royce took easily. Somehow, Royce turned around in the small space so he was straddling Shawn's head with his cock arching enticingly toward Shawn's lips as he leaned forward. It was the very definition of temptation, but Shawn waited, just eyeing the prize hanging above him until he felt the soft touch of Royce's lips circling his cock.

He gasped and arched up, desperate for more of the sublime feeling. He'd imagined this since that night in the car, and it was everything he'd pictured and more. Even with the hard shower floor beneath him, Shawn couldn't imagine a better moment. Water cascaded over Royce, drops clinging to his skin and circling around to his front and enhancing Shawn's view. He appreciated it for another moment, then lifted his head and licked the head of Royce's cock.

The water had washed away most of the dried come from the alley, but Shawn could still taste a little of the tangy flavor mixed in with the slight sweetness of the water and the saltiness of Royce's skin. The combination was unexpected but not unpleasant, and Shawn eagerly licked the length of Royce's cock before pulling back to suck just on the head.

He tried to mimic what Royce was doing, but he quickly found that if he focused on the actions, he lost the sensations and it was easier to just feel and focus on what he wanted to do with his mouth and hands. He fondled Royce's balls as he licked and sucked, then held Royce's hips to keep him in place as he took Royce all the way in.

He'd barely had a chance to get used to the sensation of Royce's cock at the back of his throat when Royce mimicked him, taking him all in one swift movement that took away the last of Shawn's ability for rational thought. His world narrowed to sensation: the patter of the shower on skin and tile, the warm wetness of Royce's mouth, the light scraping of Royce's teeth over sensitive flesh. Royce's cock filled his mouth, warm and heavy and *right*, and as he swirled his tongue and rolled his hips, Shawn was convinced this was heaven.

Shawn felt more than heard the noises Royce made, muffled as they were by the cock in his mouth and the shower raining down on them. Shawn relied on his memory of earlier instead, matching sensations to sound as he moaned and mewled around Royce's dick. He pulled his head back as far as he could, lightly scraping with his teeth, and was rewarded with an intense vibration around his cock that made him thrust upward and beg for more.

"Please," he whimpered, uncertain if Royce could hear or understand him and unable to care. He needed more, needed Royce to—Oh!

Pleasure shot through Shawn. He curled his toes and tried to hold on long enough to bring Royce over the edge with him. He clenched his hands around Royce's waist as he jerked his hips and then he was coming in Royce's mouth as he swallowed Royce's release.

When they were done, Royce rolled off and forced Shawn to scoot over so his hip was pressed against the shower wall. They lay together for a moment, gasping for breath as the water rinsed them clean, then Royce pushed up on his elbows and shook the water out of his hair. "Damn. That wasn't what I expected when I came over." He paused, looking thoughtful. "Nothing that happened tonight was expected, actually."

A knot of worry coiled in Shawn's gut, pushing at the bliss that had him still lying boneless on the shower floor. He hadn't expected anything that had happened tonight either, but he couldn't tell if Royce thought it was good, bad, or a mixture of the two. "Is that good?"

"*Very* good." Royce contorted his body into an impossible-looking position, then kicked his legs out so they were next to Shawn's and leaned down to kiss him. "God, I love you," he said, pulling back just enough to look Shawn in the eyes. "Those were the best surprises ever."

Shawn laughed as the tension in his body uncoiled, leaving him so relaxed he was glad he hadn't tried to sit up. "Don't get used to it," he said, grinning up at Royce. "I don't have a boss to tell off anymore."

Royce stood and pulled Shawn with him. "Do you think Henry knows you meant it?"

"I don't know." Shawn stepped back from Royce once he found his balance. "I need to go in to work the rest of the schedule, regardless, but I'll give my official notice tomorrow." He grabbed some shampoo and started lathering his hair. With all the time they'd just spent in the shower, he ought to come out of it clean.

"Do you think he'll want you to?" Royce took the shampoo from Shawn and started lathering his own hair. "After the way he's treated you and what you said, I'd be surprised if he wants you back."

A soap bubble fell, landing on Royce's chest, and distracted Shawn for a moment as he watched it slide down toward Royce's nipple. "If he doesn't, he doesn't," he said absently. He was done worrying about what Henry wanted. "I don't have anything else lined up yet, so I can work my schedule if he needs me to. If he doesn't…." He shrugged. "I guess I get an early start on looking for a new place to buy."

Honestly, he was trying not to think about it too hard. He would be fine and could live comfortably for some time on the money he'd saved to use as a down payment on Delicto, but that didn't make the reality any less terrifying. He'd quit his job and given up on at least part of his dream, all without having any concrete plan in place for what came next. It was as terrifying as it was exhilarating, and Shawn wasn't sure which emotion would win if he mulled for too long.

Royce made a noncommittal sound as he handed Shawn his washcloth. "You could always invest in All Corked Up. I'm going to need someone to run the restaurant part of it, and you'd be part owner. I know starting new is different from taking someplace over, but it could work."

There were a million things Shawn wanted to say to that, but he bit them all back and looked Royce square in the eyes. "We're not discussing business deals naked in the shower."

"Can we discuss them naked out of the shower?"

"*No.*" Shawn shook his head, unsure if he was exasperated or amused. Part of him wanted Royce to take this seriously, like the life-changing decision it was, but the rest of him was relieved Royce was breaking the tension and keeping him calm until they could talk about it.

Royce sighed like that was an unreasonable request. "I'm not interested in dressed and in the shower, so dressed and out of the shower it is." He looked Shawn up and down as he started washing himself. "Are you *sure* I can't persuade you to discuss this naked?"

Shawn took the opportunity to let his gaze roam over Royce's wet, soap-covered body. It was a fantastic view, one he wanted to keep looking at as long and as often as possible, but that just emphasized his point. "Do you *really* think we'd actually discuss anything if we tried to have this conversation naked? 'Cause I gotta say, our track record tonight? Not really pointing toward yes."

"Fair enough." Royce leaned in and kissed Shawn lightly on the lips. "I'm sure I can think of something to occupy my time until then."

Shawn pushed Royce under the shower spray. "We won't get dressed if you don't stop that."

Royce assumed what Shawn thought was supposed to be an innocent expression. It fell far short of that goal. "I don't know what you mean. I'd *never* try to trick you into staying naked longer."

"Well, that's disappointing." Shawn tugged Royce out from under the spray once all the soap was gone and took his place. "I usually approve of schemes to keep people naked, especially when I benefit."

"Just not tonight?"

"Just not when I have life-changing things to discuss," Shawn corrected as he turned off the water and opened the shower door. "I prefer focus for that."

Royce followed Shawn out of the shower "Well, if you don't want naked, you're going to have to lend me something. My clothes are still in the washer."

Crap. Shawn had forgotten about that. He doubted it would be much less distracting to see Royce in his clothes than to see Royce naked, but he couldn't talk about going into business with Royce while either one of them was nude. It would be impossible to take anything seriously, and for all that this felt like a spur of the moment decision, it was very serious. It was Shawn's entire future

"Right. I'll grab you something." He ignored the part of his brain that told him to wrap the towel around his waist and put it back on the rack instead. After everything he and Royce just did, there was no point in hiding anything while he went to find clothes.

He pulled out two pair of pajama bottoms and two T-shirts and handed one of each to Royce. "Here. These should work." It was hardly professional clothing, but the point was to be dressed, not dressed to the nines. The pajama bottoms and T-shirts would cover them as well as anything else in Shawn's closet and be more comfortable besides.

Royce pulled them on quickly and presented himself to Shawn with arms spread. "Do I pass inspection?"

Shawn let himself appreciate the view of Royce in his clothes for a moment before nodding. "They'll do." Royce was smaller than Shawn, so they were a little big, but not horribly so. They'd work for sitting around the apartment, at any rate. "You hungry?"

"You stalling?" Royce looked at Shawn like he'd suggested jumping out of a plane without a parachute. "Clothes, I get, but food? Really?"

"We didn't have dinner."

"True, but why don't we figure out what to do about *why* we didn't eat and then figure out dinner."

"Or we could talk while we eat." Okay, Shawn might have been stalling a little, but that didn't mean his point was invalid. They hadn't even been seated at Portland Prime before he'd had it out with Henry, and now that he wasn't focused on Royce with single-minded purpose, his stomach was making its displeasure known. "I'm not suggesting I cook a three-course meal or anything, just that we fix something quickly and eat while we talk."

"I'd like to see you cook a three-course meal," Royce said as he started toward the front of the apartment. "Can you?"

"With the recipes and the right ingredients." Shawn peered into the fridge and wrinkled his nose when he saw how empty it was. He definitely needed to go grocery shopping soon. "Tonight is beer and sandwiches, though. The three-course dinner will have to wait."

Royce helped Shawn pull cold cuts, condiments, and beer from the refrigerator. "I'm going to hold you to that. I expect a three-course meal someday."

"So long as you provide the wine."

"Of course."

They worked in silence after that, each making his own sandwich. When the food was put away and they were sitting at the table with two sandwiches and a bottle of Sam Adams each, Shawn cleared his throat. "So you really think it's a good idea for us to own a business together?"

Royce took a moment to finish chewing. "Why wouldn't it be? I need an investor, you need a place to invest in."

"It's not that simple." If that was the only factor, Shawn would put his money in All Corked Up in a heartbeat, but there was a lot more to it than that. "We'd be working together all day, every day."

"Exactly! It'll be fantastic."

"What about when we fight? What if we break up?" Shawn didn't want to think about that happening—this felt like it was forever—but he couldn't end up in another situation where he was miserable for the sake of business. "We'd still have to work together all day every day."

Royce took a swig of his beer and looked at Shawn like he'd lost his mind. "Okay, first of all, we're both adults. I think we can handle working in the same building even if we're arguing. We won't be right together all day anyway. A lot of the time, the wine shop is too busy for us to talk, and I hope the restaurant will be the same way. Plus there's always stuff to do in the office if we need a break from each other, and you'll be running the restaurant side while I run the wine shop side."

Shawn nodded. That answered his objections about them fighting, but…. "What if we break up?"

"Buy-Sell agreement." Royce picked up his sandwich and held it, ready to bite. "That's pretty standard with any business partnership. We both agree to buy the other out if one of us wants out. For whatever reason."

Shawn took a bite of his sandwich to give himself time to think. It wasn't the steak he'd been planning on tonight, but the ham was flavorful, the lettuce crisp, and the tomatoes juicy. The company was as good as he'd have gotten in the restaurant, and the appetizer certainly wasn't something they'd serve there. All in all, it had been a much better evening than the one they'd planned, and it was getting better with every objection Royce answered.

There were still a few issues, though. "What about Clint? Wasn't he going to invest in the restaurant part?"

"You investing was Clint's idea, remember?"

"Yes, but—"

"He really would rather flip a house. I promise." Royce settled back in his chair, his beer in one hand. "Besides, you investing doesn't mean Clint can't. He'll still chip in if we need him to, and he'll be an active owner too, but his dream isn't to own a wine shop or a restaurant, it's to keep flipping houses."

Shawn knew that, but it didn't stop the guilt he felt at the idea of pushing Clint out. "I'm not agreeing to anything until I talk to him. I want to make sure he's okay with it."

"I can practically guarantee he will be."

"*Practically* guarantee isn't the same as *actually* guarantee," Shawn said dryly. "Besides, I already made one life-changing decision on the spur of the moment tonight. I think I ought to sleep on this one."

Royce leaned forward, his body tense. "But you're interested?" He held up his hand as Shawn started to protest. "I'm not asking for commitment. Just tell me you're not outright rejecting it. Tell me you like the idea a little."

Shawn smiled softly, hoping to soothe some of Royce's obvious worry. "I do like the idea. I think it could be great if we can make it work. But I can't decide without thinking it over and talking to people."

"Okay." Tension bled out of Royce as he put his beer down on the table. "Since you're not going to make a decision tonight, I can think of a few *other* ways to occupy your time."

"Oh?" Shawn picked up his sandwich, took a bite, and made a deliberate show of licking a drop of mayonnaise off his lip. "Like what?"

He didn't object at all when Royce took his sandwich away and pulled him down to the floor to show him.

21

HENRY'S car was already in the parking lot at Delicto when Shawn arrived on Sunday morning. Given the confrontation the previous night, Shawn had expected Henry to arrive early, but he'd hoped to have at least a few minutes to get things started and drink a cup of coffee before he was forced into another unpleasant discussion. Clearly, that was not meant to be.

Sighing, Shawn heaved himself out of his car and glanced toward Henry's to see if Henry was waiting outside again. The Town Car was empty, so Shawn trudged into the building, wondering what he'd find inside.

Henry looked up from the desk when Shawn walked into the back. "I didn't expect to see you today."

Shawn repressed a shudder at the coolness of Henry's tone. "I told you I'd work the rest of my schedule."

"You also told me you weren't seeing that *person* anymore. You told me you wanted to buy Delicto and you'd do whatever it took to do that." Henry sneered. "Neither of those were true. Why should I believe you'll keep your word about working?"

There were so many things Shawn could say to that, but the idea of arguing again left him feeling drained. "If you don't want me here, I'll get my stuff and you'll never have to see me again. If you want me to work, then trust me to work. I'm not going to argue with you about it."

"You were happy to argue last night."

"And I'm sorry that happened the way it did, but I said everything I needed to say." Shawn sank into the chair next to the desk and pinched the bridge of his nose. It did nothing to alleviate the headache blossoming behind his eyes, but it did keep him from having to look at Henry while he talked. "I don't want to screw anyone over, so I'll work what's scheduled if you need me to, but that's it. I'm done. Whether I go now or in two weeks is up to you."

"You're really doing this?" Henry sounded like he didn't believe it. "You're really giving up on your dream? That wasn't just throwing a fit last night?"

"Owning Delicto was my dream when I thought it would make me happy, Henry," Shawn said wearily. He didn't know why he was bothering to explain. Henry would never understand. "I used to love this place, but it doesn't make me happy anymore. I'm moving on to what does."

"And when that stops making you happy? What are you going to do then? Wouldn't you rather stick with what you know?"

"No." Shawn honestly didn't see himself ever being unhappy with Royce, but even if he was someday, right now he knew he'd be miserable without him. "If I end up unhappy again, I'll find the next thing that makes me happy. I'm not going to stick with something just because I've done it for so long." He lifted his head and looked steadily at Henry. "I'm not ever going to be happy here again. I know that. And I spend way too much time working to do something that makes me miserable."

"This *boyfriend* of yours is worth it?"

"No. My happiness is worth it. He's just part of that." Shawn stood, done with the conversation and beyond ready to leave if

Henry didn't need him. "Do you want me to stay or not? I've got other places I'd rather be if you don't need me for the next two weeks."

"You're determined to do this."

"I am."

"Then go. I'll find someone to take your shifts." Henry turned back to the computer.

Shawn took that as a dismissal. "I'll get my stuff, then."

He was halfway out of the office when Henry turned around. "I hope you realize someday I was only trying to help you find the right path."

"I know you think you were." He'd known that all along. It was part of why he'd put up with as much as he had. It didn't change the things Henry had done, though, or the fact that Shawn was going to be much happier without Delicto. "I hope you realize someday there's nothing wrong with the path I chose." He doubted that would ever happen, but it wasn't his concern anymore. "Good luck, Henry. I hope everything works out for you."

Henry didn't respond, but Shawn didn't expect him to. He gathered the few things he kept in the breakroom and walked out of Delicto without another word. As the heavy doors closed behind him, they swept a weight off his shoulders, leaving him feeling lighter than he had in a long while.

The relief he felt as he crossed the parking lot wasn't unexpected, but the giddiness was. He collapsed into his car, weak-kneed at the idea he would never have to come back to Delicto again, and pulled out his phone.

The debate about who to call first was short. Royce didn't know that he didn't have to come back, but he did know about the conversation Shawn planned to have today, and he'd been there for the one last night. Anastasia didn't know about either, and Shawn needed to talk to her before he gave Royce an answer about All Corked Up.

She picked up on the first ring. "Hello?"

"I quit my job." Shawn shut the car door behind him and slid the key into the ignition. It sounded strange to say it out loud like that, like it hadn't been true until he'd spoken the words. A small bubble of hysteria rose up inside him as he started to realize what he'd actually done.

"Really?" Anastasia sounded so hopeful and excited that Shawn knew he'd made the right decision.

He swallowed a giggle. "Really."

"Do you swear? Because if you are fucking with me, Shawn Michael Neale, we are done."

"I wouldn't—" he started but stopped when Anastasia made a disbelieving noise. Once upon a time, he would have. Not since things started getting bad, though. "I swear, Stasia, I quit. I told Henry I was done last night, and I got my stuff this morning."

"I thought you had a date with Royce last night."

Of course she would remember that. "I did. It got interrupted. Let me switch over to the headset so I can drive and I'll tell you all about it."

"Sure."

Shawn pulled his headset from the center console and activated the Bluetooth on his phone. Once it connected, he turned the car on and pulled out of the parking lot. "All right. We ran into Henry and a group of his friends at Portland Prime last night, and I kind of had it out with him."

He recounted the story as he drove, ending with when they left without getting dinner. "I went in this morning to work my scheduled shifts, and Henry told me he didn't need me to."

"I don't think you're supposed to be this thrilled about being completely unemployed," Anastasia said dryly. Anyone who didn't know her would think she was displeased, but Shawn could tell she was happy for him.

"I don't know," he said impishly, "I think it's great. I don't have any place I have to be, don't have any responsibilities…."

"Don't have any way to pay your bills…." Anastasia chuckled. "Well, I know you do for a while, but you're going to have to find something eventually."

"I think I know what I'm going to do about that, actually." Shawn pulled into a grocery store parking lot and parked near the back. He'd wanted to get away from Delicto, but he didn't want to have this discussion while he was driving. If it took as long as he thought it might, he'd reach All Corked Up before he was done, and he didn't want that either. "Royce is expanding the shop to include a restaurant, and he asked me to go in on it with him. I'd be part owner and mostly run the restaurant side and he'd mostly run the wine shop part."

Anastasia got quiet for a moment. "Do you think that's a good idea?"

"I was hoping you'd tell me." Shawn laughed shakily. "It's practically a dream come true. I won't have to worry about finding a place to buy or spending all the money I have saved until I do. I'd get to build the brand instead of being trapped into whatever place I buy. I'd get to work with my boyfriend."

"Okay…." Anastasia drew the word out. "Sounds fantastic. What's the downside?"

"There isn't one." Shawn didn't quite believe it, but he'd spent most of the night thinking about it and he hadn't been able to come up with one. "We talked about what would happen if we broke up and we can handle it like any other business partnership. I'm going to talk to Clint to be sure he meant it when he suggested I invest instead of him, but other than that, I haven't been able to think of anything."

"What's Clint going to do if he doesn't invest?"

"Buy another house to flip." Personally, Shawn found the idea of constantly doing construction tedious, but he could see how Clint liked it. "He flips a few every year. Apparently he was holding off on the next one in case Royce needed him to invest, but if I do, he won't need to."

"Huh. Interesting." Something in Anastasia's voice made Shawn wonder what she was thinking, but she clearly wasn't going to tell him now. "So why haven't you agreed to this already? You two should be halfway to the bank to sign paperwork by now!"

"It's almost too perfect. What if something goes wrong?"

"It's life. Stuff's gonna go wrong. Is there a bigger chance this will crash and burn than anything else you'd invest in?"

"No. Just a bigger chance I'll get hurt if it does."

Anastasia chuckled. "Royce is a good guy. I think you'll be fine. And if I'm wrong and you lose everything, I promise I'll beat him up for you and let you live on my couch for as long as you need."

The offer was utterly ridiculous, but it solidified Shawn's decision for him. "Gee, thanks, Stasia. Just what I need. You beating up my boyfriend will get me all the cool boys."

"I promise not to beat him up until he's an ex-boyfriend," she said primly. "Now go, make sure Clint was serious, and tell Royce you want to own a restaurant with him."

Shawn started the car again. "I'm going! I'm going!"

"Good." Anastasia paused just long enough for Shawn to wonder if she was going to hang up. "So what are you going to do with the place?"

Shawn laughed. He didn't have any concrete ideas, but he started talking about things that had crossed his mind at one point or another for Delicto and how they might apply to All Corked Up. Before he knew it, he was parked and trying to get Anastasia off the phone as he walked into the building.

Clint was behind the counter. He watched in amusement as Shawn finished the call and smirked when he hung up. "She's tenacious."

"Like you're one to talk."

Clint nodded in agreement. "True. Royce is upstairs. You can go and knock at the top if you want."

"In a minute. I actually wanted to ask you something first."

"Shoot."

Shawn shifted, suddenly nervous. If Clint didn't give him the answer he was expecting, it would throw all his plans out of whack. "When you said I should invest in the restaurant with Royce instead of you, did you mean it?"

"Yeah," Clint said as though Shawn should have known better than to ask. "I'd much rather flip houses than run a restaurant."

Shawn let out the breath he hadn't known he was holding and grinned in relief. "Awesome. Thanks."

"You're welcome?" Clint clearly didn't know what he was being thanked for. Shawn waited a beat, confident he'd figure it out, and wasn't disappointed. Clint's eyes widened comically and he leaned over the counter. "Wait. Does this mean you're going to?"

Shawn smirked and headed toward the back. "I think I should give Royce my answer before I let you know, don't you?"

"That's a yes!"

"Maybe." It was, but Shawn wasn't going to tell Clint that. Instead, he slipped through the door in the back and closed it behind him so Clint wouldn't overhear the conversation. The door at the top of the stairs was closed, so Shawn knocked softly. "Royce?"

"It's open!"

Shawn opened the door carefully, looking out for escaping cats, but neither Puck nor Kirra was anywhere to be seen when he stepped through. Curious, Shawn looked around, but he didn't see any sign of Royce either, and he frowned as he shut the door. "Royce?" He'd been here enough now that he knew the layout of the apartment, but he still felt awkward wandering around by himself. "Where are you?"

"In the office!" This time, Royce was easier to hear. Shawn followed the sound down the hall to the room Royce had pointed to the last time he was over but that he'd never been in. Today, the door was open and Royce was sitting at a desk in front of a window, his side to the door, doing something on the computer.

Shawn leaned against the doorframe and watched him for a moment, appreciating the way his nose twitched as he scowled at the screen. "Hey."

"Hi!" Royce immediately brightened, his nose stilling and the crinkles around his eyes deepening. "I didn't think I'd see you for a while." He'd stayed the night at Shawn's after they'd christened both the kitchen floor and the couch, but Shawn had kicked him out early so he could get to work, and he hadn't planned on being free for several hours yet. "I thought you had to work."

"Not anymore." It came out sounding a little more bitter than Shawn had intended, and he was surprised to realize he was genuinely upset by Henry's decision. He really hadn't wanted to work the next two weeks at a place he hated, but he didn't like not leaving on his own terms, either. "If I'm not in it for the long haul, Henry doesn't want me around, apparently."

"Jesus." Royce came over, took Shawn's hand, and rubbed his thumb along the back in a comforting gesture. "What did he say?"

"The same old. He said he was surprised I'd showed up since I didn't keep my word about not dating you or about buying Delicto, and then he tried to convince me—again—that I'd be better off sticking where I was and adhering to his rules." Shawn shuddered at the memory and squeezed Royce's hand for comfort. "He tried to tell me that I might not be happy with you forever, so I should give up on the idea and stay with the devil I know. He seems to think that long-term misery is better than happiness if it's not going to last forever."

"That's stupid." Royce rolled his eyes as he let go of Shawn's hand and flopped back in his chair. "Why would you want to be miserable all the time?"

"Fuck if I know." Shawn slumped into the room's other chair. "He told me that he hoped someday I'd realize he was only looking out for me." He snorted, unamused. "I told him I hoped someday he'd realize there was nothing wrong with my choices."

"Good." Royce stretched his foot out and bumped it against Shawn's. "So, what, he just told you not to come back?"

"After failing to convince me I was wrong, yep." Shawn hooked his foot around Royce's and tried to smile. "So I guess I get to start my new career a little sooner than I'd planned."

"And what *is* your new career?" Royce looked hopeful, but sobered almost instantly. "If you've decided, that is. I'm not trying to pressure you."

Shawn considered teasing him, but he'd already made his decision, and it would be mean to make Royce wait any longer for his answer. He leaned forward, rested his elbows on his knees, and smiled. For all that he'd worried about changing his entire life and wondered what would happen when he stood up to Henry, telling Royce was surprisingly easy. "I'm in."

Royce's blinding smile was the best answer he could have received.

Epilogue

ROYCE fingered the key in his pocket as they drove away from the lawyer, where they'd signed the last of the paperwork required to make Shawn co-owner of All Corked Up and secure the funding and permits to begin the expansion. He'd been carrying it with him ever since that Sunday Shawn had showed up in his office and told him he wanted to invest, but he hadn't yet found the right time to give it to Shawn. Now that everything was final, he had no excuse to delay any longer.

Shawn pulled the car into the lot at the store and parked in the spot next to Royce's, now reserved for him. Royce had put the sign up just yesterday, and the concrete proof that Shawn would be there often enough to get his own special spot made Royce giddy every time he looked at it. Even now, with everything signed and official, he had a hard time believing Shawn had agreed to do this with him. It seemed surreal, like a dream, but the little bits of tangible proof reminded him it was reality.

He slipped out of the car quickly and hurried to the door. Shawn joined him a moment later and laughed as he slid his arms around Royce's waist from behind. "Anxious to get inside your store?"

"*Our* store," Royce corrected, unable to keep from grinning. He pulled the key out of his pocket and pressed it into Shawn's hand. "Would you like to do the honors?"

Shawn looked at the key over Royce's shoulder and stepped out from behind him with a stunned look on his face. "Our store, huh?"

"That is what all that paperwork we signed was about, wasn't it?" Royce shook his hand in an exaggerated manner and winced at the memory of the number of pages he'd signed. With all the various things they'd had to take care of to make this final, he had honestly felt like he was signing his life away instead of setting it up for something great. "I hope it was, because otherwise I gave myself a hand cramp for no reason."

"It was." The stunned look faded from Shawn's face, replaced by one of pleased awe. "Our store, then. And I would love to do the honors."

The look on Shawn's face as he opened the door reminded Royce of the feeling he'd had when he'd first bought the store. He could still remember the amazement he'd felt when he'd walked in and realized this was all his, even though it had only been an empty room at the time. Now it was a thriving wine shop, but the promise of more and the idea that he'd get to do it with Shawn was almost as exhilarating.

Shawn turned around in a full circle after he stepped through the door, his smile bigger than Royce had ever seen it. "It feels different."

"I know." Royce stepped up behind Shawn and wrapped his arms around his waist, mimicking Shawn's pose from earlier. "Owning it makes a difference."

"Yeah, but it's not that. Or not just that, anyway." Shawn spun around again, twisting out of Royce's grip. "I see possibilities now. And problems," he admitted slightly more wryly. "But mostly possibilities. There were so many things I wanted to do with Delicto, but I never would've been able to, even after Henry sold it. They just wouldn't work with the building or the business or the staff. But here, we're starting fresh on everything, and we can do whatever we want."

"Not completely fresh," Royce said. "We're not getting rid of my employees."

"I know Clint and the girls are here to stay. But we're going to hire new staff for the restaurant. We're going to renovate the unused part of the building. And we can give it whatever vibe we want, so long as it doesn't clash with the wine shop."

"I don't think much would clash with the vibe All Corked Up already has."

"A prissy place would, but nothing either of us will want to do." Shawn walked over to the entrance to the other room. "I was thinking we could put conversation-style seating in this room. We can keep the bar to be used during tastings, and maybe set up something so that people can get wine from it when they're sitting in here too? They could eat in here with a small menu, or get the full menu in the restaurant part."

It was a good idea. Royce nodded thoughtfully as he joined Shawn. "Maybe. We have to figure out how to keep the cats out, though. Having them run around is part of the character of the shop, but if we're serving food, they can't be down here. I had been thinking we'd build a door between this area and the restaurant so they couldn't get through, but we'd have to modify things a little more if we're going to serve food in here too."

"True." Shawn shrugged and looked around again. "We'll have to talk about it. I'm sure there's *something* we can do."

"We can do whatever we want," Royce reminded him. "If we have to, I can start keeping the cats upstairs."

"We'll figure it out. I have ideas for the restaurant part too, but there's something we need to do before we talk about them."

"What?" Royce could think of several things, but he was curious what Shawn's idea was. "Get blueprints? Talk to Clint since he's the one with experience renovating? Look at the building permits and figure out what, exactly, we're allowed to do to the building? Announce the upcoming renovations so our customers aren't surprised?"

"All of that." Shawn took Royce's hand and led him back into the front room of the shop. "But *first*, we should celebrate."

"With wine?" Royce suggested in an innocent tone. He knew what Shawn was suggesting, but he wanted to tease a little. "I have some special bottles I keep in the back that would be perfect."

"While I *fully* support the idea of celebrating with alcohol, it's a little early in the day for that, don't you think? It isn't even eleven yet."

"It's five o'clock somewhere."

Shawn rolled his eyes at the cheesy line, but his expression remained fond. "It isn't here. Besides, I think we should save the wine for later. We can share it with Stasia and Clint. We're *not* sharing what I have in mind." He leaned in close to Royce's ear. "And if we're going upstairs, we should leave before Clint gets here to open the shop. You know he'll want details if he sees us go up."

"True." As much as Royce would have enjoyed breaking out one of his special bottles of wine, he knew he'd enjoy taking Shawn upstairs and celebrating properly even more. Clint would probably pry about how they celebrated regardless, but if he didn't watch them escape upstairs, he probably wouldn't ask with Shawn around, and that was better than the alternative.

He led the way upstairs, shooed the cats down into the shop so they wouldn't interrupt, and pulled Shawn into the bedroom. "Now. You said something about celebrating?"

Shawn grinned wickedly in response. "I did." He started unbuttoning Royce's dress shirt. "I think I should start by stripping you naked, pinning you to the bed, and having my way with you."

Royce's breath caught in his throat, and he nodded fervently in agreement. If that was Shawn's idea of a good celebration, he'd have to be sure they marked every milestone in their relationship and their business. He could think of a few more just off the top of his head, and he couldn't wait to see what sort of things they ended up celebrating as they expanded All Corked Up together. "Sounds perfect."

NESSA L. WARIN lives in a fantasy world that's mostly inside her head, though her physical address is in southwestern Ohio. Her two cats kindly play along with her fantasies and graciously let her pay all the bills, but they do require her to provide pampering on a regular basis. Nessa enjoys exploring the wonders of this world through travel—something her cats strongly disapprove of as it cuts into their pampering time—and can find whimsy in the most mundane places. When the real world becomes too much, Nessa enjoys dressing in costume and going to Renaissance Festivals and fantasy conventions. A short trip to either does wonders for her state of mind, so she makes sure to attend at least one of each every year. These trips help Nessa add to her collection of faerie and dragon art, and she swears she will frame and hang all the prints she's collected some time soon.

When she's not living in a fantasy world, Nessa enjoys tasting and learning about wine, particularly since it's one of the few things she and the rest of her family agree on. She's a regular at the wine tastings held by her local wine shop, and considers it a sin for her wine rack to have more empty spots than full ones. She'd prefer her wine rack to be filled with Pinot Noir, Malbec, and Syrah, but one of her favorite things about wine is the way it can always surprise her. More than once she's been taken aback by which wine she likes best at a tasting, and she loves the way her wine rack illustrates the joys of trying new things.

Follow Nessa on Twitter @nessalwarin and Facebook at NessaLWarin. She can also be reached at nessa.l.warin@gmail.com.

Also by NESSA L. WARIN

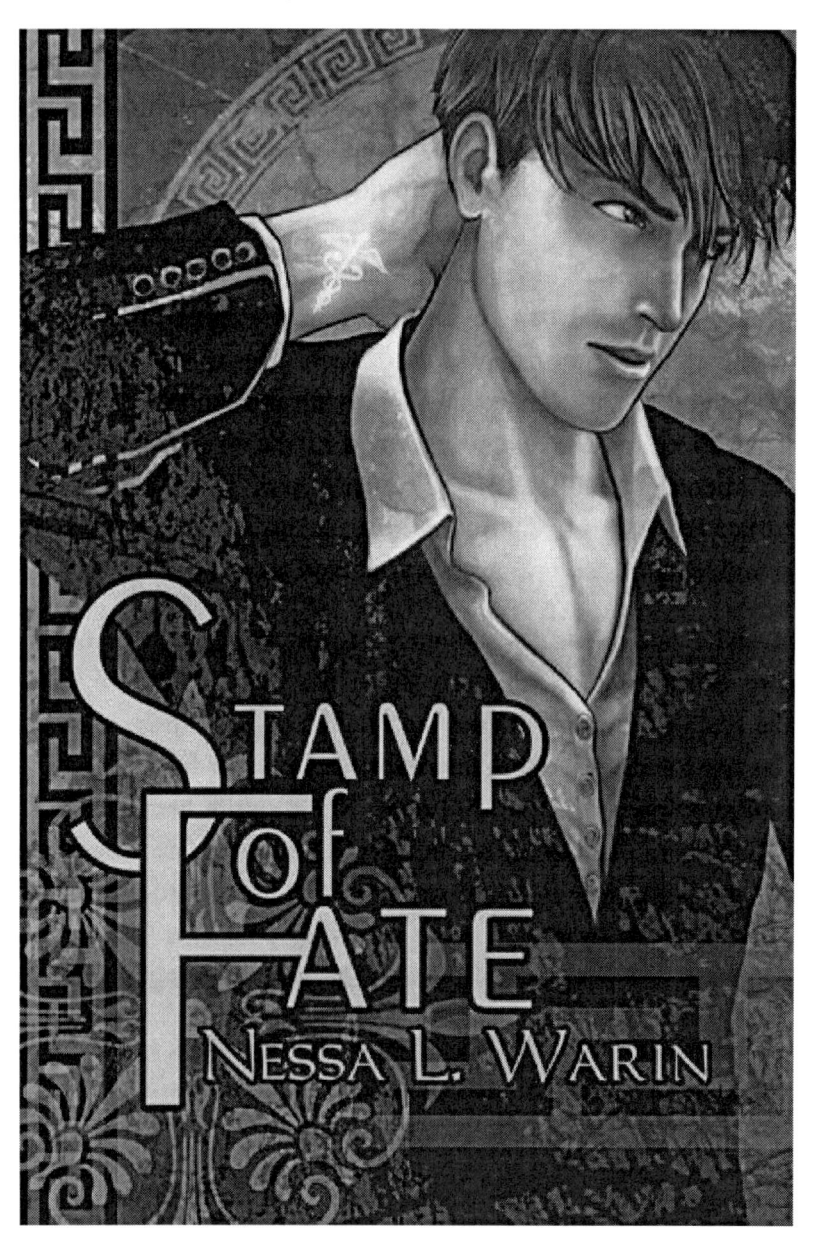

STAMP of FATE
NESSA L. WARIN

http://www.dreamspinnerpress.com